"If Babies Bother You, Just Knock And I'll See What I Can Do. But I Can't Make Any Promises."

J.J. blinked at Jack, feeling like a batter with too many balls being pitched at once. "Babies? What babies?"

"My babies. I've got three of them."

Jack Remington with *babies*. What a concept. Poor little things. *"You* have babies?" she echoed incredulously.

He nodded, his eyes smiling. "It's pretty standard. Lots of people have little ones. It's an accepted practice, even in these modern times."

"Not everyone does it," she said, realizing her tone was defensive and regretting it.

"No, of course not." His eyes narrowed, as though something in her voice piqued his interest. "Nice meeting you, Miss Jensen." Grinning, he waved and went on his way.

Jack Remington. Of all the people to run into. And he hadn't even remembered her.

Dear Reader,

Established stars and exciting new names...that's what's in store for you this month from Silhouette Desire. Let's begin with Cait London's MAN OF THE MONTH, *Tallchief's Bride*—it's also the latest in her wonderful series, THE TALLCHIEFS.

The fun continues with *Babies by the Busload*, the next book in Raye Morgan's THE BABY SHOWER series, and *Michael's Baby*, the first installment of Cathie Linz's delightful series, THREE WEDDINGS AND A GIFT.

So many of you have indicated how much you love the work of Peggy Moreland, so I know you'll all be excited about her latest sensuous romp, *A Willful Marriage*. And Anne Eames, who made her debut earlier in the year in Silhouette Desire's Celebration 1000, gives us more pleasure with *You're What?!* And if you enjoy a little melodrama with your romance, take a peek at Metsy Hingle's enthralling new book, *Backfire*.

As always, each and every Silhouette Desire is sensuous, emotional and sure to leave you feeling good at the end of the day!

Happy Reading!

Lucia Macro

Senior Editor

Please address questions and book requests to:
Silhouette Reader Service
U.S.: 3010 Walden Ave., P.O. Box 1325, Buffalo, NY 14269
Canadian: P.O. Box 609, Fort Erie, Ont. L2A 5X3

RAYE MORGAN

BABIES BY THE BUSLOAD

SILHOUETTE *Desire*

Published by Silhouette Books

America's Publisher of Contemporary Romance

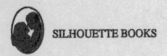

SILHOUETTE BOOKS

ISBN 0-373-76022-1

BABIES BY THE BUSLOAD

Books by Raye Morgan

Silhouette Desire

Embers of the Sun #52
Summer Wind #101
Crystal Blue Horizon #141
A Lucky Streak #393
Husband for Hire #434
Too Many Babies #543
Ladies' Man #562
In a Marrying Mood #623
Baby Aboard #673
Almost a Bride #717
The Bachelor #768
Caution: Charm at Work #807
Yesterday's Outlaw #836
The Daddy Due Date #843
Babies on the Doorstep #886
Sorry, the Bride Has Escaped #892
*Baby Dreams #997
*A Gift for Baby #1010
*Babies by the Busload #1022

*The Baby Shower

Silhouette Romance

Roses Never Fade #427

RAYE MORGAN

favors settings in the West, which is where she has spent most of her life. She admits to a penchant for Western heroes, believing that whether he's a rugged outdoorsman or a smooth city sophisticate, he tends to have a streak of wildness that the romantic heroine can't resist taming. She's been married to one of those Western men for twenty years and is busy raising four more in her Southern California home.

The Invitation

This is your last chance, J.J.

Mike's voice echoed in her mind again and again until she was sick to death of it.

This is your last chance, J.J.

Closing her eyes, she lay back in the water of the outdoor deck hot tub and tried to block the voice out of her head. Remembering it certainly wasn't doing anything for her self-esteem and she was going to need all her confidence if she was going to parlay this temporary job at a local television station into a step up that slippery ladder she'd been trying to climb for the past ten years.

Today had been a pretty pathetic attempt. Despite everything, she had to laugh when she thought about it. During the course of the morning, she'd spilled coffee down the front of her only good suit, eaten the last doughnut just before the station manager came looking for it, and called the mayor of the city by his rival's name on camera.

She had to go back tonight for the evening news, and she wasn't looking forward to it. Maybe, she thought ruefully, she should fill up on food before she went. If she could just stay away from snacks this evening, maybe things would go better.

"No," she said sadly, shaking her head at a bird who was hovering close and considering her with a glint in its eyes. "The station manager hates me. The next three weeks are going to be murder, whether I eat or not."

The bird flew off and she laughed softly, enjoying this outdoor retreat, enjoying the clouds scudding past, the wind in the pines over her head, glad she was going to get to stay here for the next five weeks.

Five weeks. That was what they'd said when they asked her to come in as a replacement anchor for a local woman who was going to be out with surgery. She'd jumped at the chance for a change. Her contract was up at the station in Sacramento, where she'd been for four years, and she knew the only way she was going to get back on track toward New York and the networks was to move around, get noticed. So here she was in St. Johns, Utah, staying in a condo the station had obtained for her, and hoping for great things.

Closing her eyes again, she turned on the jets with her toes and let herself drift in the lovely bubbles, trying to forget her agent's voice, trying to relax. The jets made just enough noise so that she didn't hear her visitor until he was standing at the edge of her deck, clearing his throat.

Her eyes flew open and so did her mouth. "Aaaah!" she shrieked, and she lost her bearings in the spa, slipping off the seat and down under the water with a thunk.

She'd barely had time to register the fact that there was a man in her yard. Fighting her way back to the surface of the water, she hoped against hope it had been a mirage.

But no. The man still stood there, smiling casually, his hands in his pockets. He was tall, his rakishly combed dark hair touched with silver at the temples, and he was wearing an Irish fisherman's sweater and slacks with wet spots on the legs. It seemed she'd created something of a splash going down.

"Sorry to startle you," he said mildly, amusement glinting in his blue eyes. "I brought you your mail."

J.J. stared out through a curtain of wet hair, blowing bubbles off her lips so that she could speak.

"Who are you?" she croaked, thanking her lucky stars that she'd had the presence of mind to put on a swimsuit instead of bathing in the buff, as had been her first inclination.

"Oh, that's right. We haven't met." He stepped up onto the redwood deck, leaned toward her and stuck his hand out quite pleasantly. "I'm Jack. I live next door."

She was beet red and she knew it. Ignoring his offered hand, she glared at him. "You shouldn't creep up on people like that," she protested.

Withdrawing his hand, he smiled as though to reassure her that there would be no hard feelings over her rudeness. "I didn't creep, exactly. There's a well-used gate between our yards. And I thought I heard voices, so I came on over."

He shook his head as though it were just the most natural thing in the world.

"The previous tenant and I had...a sort of arrangement," he explained carelessly, glancing toward the sliding glass doors that led into the house. "I guess I got used to being a little too free with her living space. Sorry." He glanced at her again and gave her another utterly charming smile.

"So you're the latest," he said softly, looking her over.

She blinked at him. "The latest what?"

He shrugged. "The latest neighbor," he said smoothly, but she knew very well that wasn't what he'd begun to say. What was special about her staying in this condo? She frowned. She was going to have to look into that.

"Lovely view, isn't it?" he added, making a sweeping motion with his arm.

She nodded, glancing at the stately pines and the vista of the red rock mountains behind the condos. The afternoon air was cool at this time of year in southern Utah, but the sun was shining and the water was scalding, and she could make believe she was in a mountain spring, absorbing nature with every pore. She loved it. But she hadn't counted on visitors sharing the experience with her.

And there was something else. She stared up at him. That voice. There was something about this man....

"Anyway, as I said, I brought your mail." He pulled a pink envelope out of his pocket. "The postman put it in my box. I'm afraid I opened it before I realized it wasn't for me."

He'd said his name was Jack. Jack. Yes, it rang a bell. She was certain she'd seen him before, perhaps a younger version.

He was waving the envelope at her. "You seem to be invited to a baby shower," he told her helpfully, leaning back against the wall with one leg bent casually over the other as he studied the paper in his hand. "Some old friend. Let's see, her name was ... ah, here it is. Sara." He looked at her questioningly, one dark eyebrow cocked provocatively. "Anyone you know?"

"Hey," she said, suddenly realizing what he was doing. "That's my mail you're reading."

His glance was laced with amusement. "Yes, I thought I'd said that. It is the whole point of my stopping by, after all."

She frowned at him, still too stunned by his behavior to get herself into the proper mode to repel his unwelcome visit. "I can read my own mail."

"Not while you're wet," he said sensibly. "I'm just trying to be helpful."

There was something about this man, something...

Jack Remington.

Oh my God, her inner child cried as the name flashed into her mind. *No, not Jack Remington!*

"The postmark says Denver," he said. "What a coincidence. I'm going to Denver myself soon."

"How nice," she said crisply, finally reasserting herself and applying a quick hand to her dark hair, pushing it back off her face. "Thank you for dropping by my mail. Now if you don't mind, I'd like some privacy."

"Of course." He straightened. "Well, nice meeting you, Miss..." He glanced at the name on the envelope before he set it down on the deck. "Miss J. J. Jensen. I guess I've worn out my welcome."

She didn't contradict him. Jack Remington. Now that she'd realized who he was, she didn't know how she could have hesitated. Talk about a blast from the past. This was a major blow.

He stopped just inside the gate to the next yard, turning back. "By the way," he noted. "If the babies bother you, just knock on the wall and I'll see what I can do. But I can't make any promises."

She blinked, frowning, feeling like a batter with too many balls being pitched at once. "Babies? What babies?"

"My babies. I've got three of them."

Jack Remington with babies. What a concept. The poor little things. "*You* have babies?" she echoed incredulously.

He nodded, his eyes smiling. "It's a pretty standard thing to do. People get married, have little ones. It's an accepted practice, even in these modern times."

Maybe for some. "Not everyone does it," she said, realizing her tone was defensive and regretting it, but it was only natural. She was so sick of people asking when she was going to "settle down."

"No, of course not." His eyes narrowed as though something in her voice had piqued his interest. "Nice meeting you, Miss Jensen." Grinning, he waved and went on his way.

She held her breath until she heard a sound that could be his gate closing, and then she stepped tentatively out of the tub, reaching quickly for her towel. Jack Remington. Of all people to run into. And he hadn't recognized her, even when he'd seen her name. That just showed how little he'd ever noticed.

Hugging the towel in close around her, she felt that old hollow feeling in the pit of her stomach, as though her world were crashing down around her. Things were changing so quickly, and lately everything new that happened seemed to be a bad thing. This was a time in her life when she should be moving forward, not stumbling backward. This just wasn't right.

And now she'd been accosted in her hot tub by the only man who had ever fired her.

So far, anyway. She made a face at her reflection in the mirror. The way things were going, who knew? A picture of the station manager's furious face when he'd found out his doughnut was missing swam into her mind. So far.

But that was not the overriding issue of the moment. Picking up the invitation, she pulled it out of the envelope and looked at it, feeling a bittersweet smile coming on. Sara's baby shower. All her old roommates from college would be there and they were all doing so well. Cami was publishing a scientific journal of some sort. Hailey was a buyer for a major department store and selling a few paintings on the side. Sara was married to the perfect man and no doubt having the perfect baby.

And here was J.J., still searching for success. How was she going to keep a smile on her face and pretend she was just as happy as the others? She wanted to see her friends again, but something deep inside resisted. If only she could go without feeling like a failure. If only.

Still, she would go if she could get the time off. She had to.

A sound from next door swung her head around. A baby was crying, then a voice, then a child's laugh. Jack Remington, playboy and man-about-town with babies? And what sort of wife, she wondered? It was going to be interesting finding out.

One

Jack Remington was floating just on the edge of sleep. Light was coming in through the slats in the blinds. Morning. Time for the madness to begin again. He listened, but the only sound came from the black cat curled at the foot of his bed, purring like a small and very loud generator.

Slowly he forced his eyes to open and listened a little harder. Nope, no sign of the babies. They were either still asleep, which was highly unusual, or they'd knotted together sheets and escaped out their window in the dead of night. Since they were only eleven months old, it seemed a long shot.

"And yet, one can always hope," he muttered to himself groggily, but he grimaced as he said the words, knowing he didn't mean them.

His dark gaze traveled around the room and lingered for a reluctant moment on the picture sitting atop the chest of drawers across the room and he frowned, repressing the twinge of pain that always cut deep when he remembered his wife. Every time it happened, he vowed to put that picture away in a drawer somewhere. But somehow he couldn't do it. Not yet.

For some reason that made him think of his new neighbor. Quite a contrast to his elegant Phoebe was Miss J. J. Jensen, with her neon string bikini and her hair plastered over her face. He grinned, thinking of the way she'd splashed about in the hot tub the day before. He had to admit she'd been a fetching sight. Nice breasts, from what he could see amid all that splashing—the sort of body that made a man think twice about this celibacy kick he'd been on for so long.

"Daddy?"

Annie was in the bedroom doorway that he always left open so as to hear every sound from the babies' room. She peered at her father around two small fists that were rubbing the sand from her eyes.

"Daddy, the babies are still sleeping," she whispered in a tone that could have jerked Rip van Winkle out of a sound sleep.

Propping up on one elbow, he put a finger to his lips to quiet her and then gave her a daddy-sized grin. She was the best antidote he knew of for stray thoughts about attractive women. When in doubt, he could always count on his little Annie to bring him back down to earth and remind him of what was important in his life.

"What do we always say, Annie-kins?" he asked.

She furled her young brow and thought hard. "Let sleeping babies lie?" she guessed correctly, her brown eyes huge.

He nodded, pleased with her, as always. Five years old and going on middle age, she had a natural wisdom that often stunned him.

"Come here and give me my morning bear hug, you little rascal," he demanded tenderly, and she flew across the hardwood floor, her white nightgown billowing around her, her blond curls bouncing, and threw her arms around his neck, squeezing hard and giving him a pretend growl.

He laughed as she let go, giggling. "Best bear hug yet, Annie," he told her. "You nearly took my head off."

She smiled happily and turned to dash off again, but not before stopping to shake her finger at the dozing cat.

"Gregor, you are making a very big noise," she whispered loudly to the startled animal. "Shh, you'll wake up the babies."

Gregor stretched out his front legs and yawned, and Annie went on her way. Jack chuckled, enjoying the sunny domestic scene, but his smile faded as his thoughts grew darker. This situation wasn't really fair to Annie, and he was going to have to think about ways to remedy it. They were an odd little family, he and the triplets and five-year-old Annie. And then there was Marguerite.

Annie's little feet made a pattern on the hallway floor as she returned, her eyes wider than ever. "Daddy, Marguerite is already up," she announced breathlessly. "She's cooking something."

"Uh-oh." Jack groaned. "What is it? Could you tell?"

Annie made a face. "I think it's pancakes."

"Oh." He brightened. "Great. Her pancakes aren't half-bad."

Annie frowned, looking worried. "But Daddy...what if she puts those little blue balls in?"

He blinked at her. "Blueberries? They're great."

Her lip curled dramatically. "They're yucky."

He laughed shortly. "Don't you tell her that. Remember, we love Marguerite's cooking, no matter what. You got it?"

She nodded reluctantly. "I got it," she echoed, her voice as sad as her eyes.

He sighed and lay back against the pillow for one last moment, his arms behind his head. Marguerite was in the kitchen. Now he was going to have to get up. What did you call it when the hired help made almost as many problems as she solved? A dilemma, at the very least.

He glanced down at his daughter. "Okay, I'm getting up. You go get dressed and we'll meet in the kitchen, okay? And whatever it is that Marguerite's cooking, we're going to love it. Right?"

Annie made a face, her teeth on edge, and dashed off toward her own room to change. Jack willed his body to rise, and surprisingly, it did as he asked, but it creaked along the way.

"Getting to be an old man at thirty-five," he muttered as he made his way to the shower. "Raising babies saps the strength right out of you."

As if on cue, the first sounds from the babies' room came wafting in through the doorway, and he hesitated, then opted for a quick shower before going to them. And quick it was. He barely lasted long enough for the drops to hit his skin before he was back out, toweling down and hurrying to reach the babies. For just a moment he had fleeting thoughts of the old days when he'd luxuriated in a warm shower, letting the stinging drops hit him for minutes at a time. Those days were gone. Now it was slapdash and make it faster. The babies called.

For just a moment, the image of his new neighbor spun into view again. She'd seemed to have plenty of time to wallow in her hot tub. He remembered when he'd been young like that, with every possible path still in front of him, and for a brief moment, he envied her.

But he quickly shoved the thought away. He couldn't let stray impulses cloud his horizon. He'd made a commitment to these kids and he was going to keep it, even if everyone on earth seemed to think he was nuts.

"Give a couple of them up for adoption," someone had actually suggested. "You can't possibly take care of all four at once by yourself."

"Send them home to your mother" was another refrain he often heard.

"Don't they have child-care professionals who can come in and take over running the house and raising the kids so you won't have to?" said another helpful soul.

He'd reacted to every such comment with good-natured humor on the outside, and outraged horror on the inside. These were his kids. They'd already lost a mother. There was no way they were going to have to be raised without a father—a one hundred percent, there-for-you-whenever-you-need-him father.

So, despite the attractions living right next door, there would be no lusting after beautiful neighbors. Indulging himself in that sort of thing would bring disaster, and he wasn't going to do it, not even for a moment.

But the time for thought evaporated as his day began at its usual frantic pace. Marguerite's voice was calling him, and so were the voices from the next room.

"Mister? Mister?" Marguerite shouted from the kitchen. "I got you food ready. It gonna get cold!"

He hopped on one foot as he wrestled with his slacks. "You'll have to keep it warm for me, Marguerite," he called. "The babies are awake."

The banging of pans was her only answer, and he winced, but he went in to see his little ones. Three cribs lined one wall, three mobiles hung over them and three little children were each standing up and leaning on the railings, little fingers curled around the edge.

Three. It always gave him a beat of panic when he saw them like this, their sweet round faces gazing at him eagerly. They wanted so much, needed so much. How could anyone possibly minister to three at once? It was impossible. But somehow, he had to try.

He got to work quickly, swinging up the first baby and heading for the changing table. Annie arrived, dressed in jeans and a little red shirt, and pitched in as she always did. Jack spoke softly to each baby as he cleaned and changed and dressed him or her. Luckily they were usually good-natured in the morning, cooing and laughing while Annie amused them. Still, it was half an hour later before they were through. He hurried out to the kitchen with one baby under each arm, while Annie lugged the third one.

All seemed quiet on the cooking front. Marguerite was nowhere to be seen, but two plates of cold pancakes sat at nicely set places at the table, and three dishes of congealed oatmeal sat on the counter. Jack took in the situation at a glance and, knowing his hired help, plunked his two babies down in walkers and motioned for Annie to do the same with hers. He knew the babies were hungry, but they would have to wait. There were times when a man had to do what a man had to do.

"Sit down, quick," he whispered to Annie. "We'll eat and then feed the little ones."

The babies had no problem with the order of things. They were gurgling with laughter and careening together in their walkers like little round bumper cars. Meanwhile, Jack poured syrup over his pancakes and said very loudly, "Wow, these are really good. Marguerite sure knows how to fix a good breakfast, doesn't she, Annie?"

Annie sat on the edge of her chair and stared down at the plate before her. There were blueberries in the pancakes.

Jack saw her look and gave her an encouraging smile. "All together now," he urged under his breath. "We love it!" he said aloud. "Don't we, Annie?"

Annie mouthed the words but her heart wasn't in it and rebellion brewed in her brown eyes. Still she managed to put a bite into her mouth by the time Marguerite reappeared, looking at them suspiciously, her green eyes darting a glance from one plate to another. Her blond hair was a little wild this morning and her thick, shapeless body was rendered even more lumplike by the plain housedress she wore. A woman of middle years, she had seemingly lost all interest in looking attractive.

"Marguerite, these are the best pancakes you've made yet," Jack lied, raising his voice to be heard over the din of the babies attacking each other with the walkers. "Delicious."

Marguerite's face began to relax. "You really like?" she asked hopefully.

Jack nodded. "Great stuff," he said with his mouth full.

Marguerite smiled. "Okay. I warm up this oatmeal for the babies, okay? Then I help you feed them."

Jack felt the tension in his shoulders let go just a little bit. She wasn't going to quit this morning at any rate.

"That would be wonderful," he said with real conviction. He took another huge bite of the cold pancakes and she smiled more happily, dusting her hands against her white apron.

"Okay," she said again, bustling about the stove. "Okay."

Jack glanced at Annie. She was still chewing on her original bite, her face filled with tragedy. He opened his mouth to say something to her, but before he got the words out, one of the baby walkers crashed into another a little too hard and both babies began to shriek. He jumped up to take care of things, but something inside was beginning to feel the same rebellion he'd seen in Annie's eyes. There was a part of him that would have jumped at the chance to run off with . . . say, the nicely proportioned neighbor he'd met the day before in her hot tub. Run off with her to some nice warm beach in the tropics and laze the day away.

But that wasn't going to happen. He pulled his baby up into his arms and sighed, cuddling and comforting. No, that wasn't going to happen for a long time. Maybe for eighteen years or so, the way things were going.

Two

J.J. felt like whistling as she walked up the pathway to her condo. Things had gone much better today. The gift-wrapped box of special doughnuts she'd brought in for the station manager seemed to have done the trick of turning him from a foe into a fan. And when she'd had a chance to fill in and do a morning update, there had been a flurry of complimentary phone calls from the public. Things were looking up, and she smiled to herself as she fumbled for her keys, shifting from one hand to the other the bag of groceries she'd picked up on her way home.

A feeling rather than a sound prickled the nerve endings on the back of her neck, and she looked around to find a young girl sitting on the steps to the next condo, gazing at her solemnly.

"Hi," J.J. said, surprised. She didn't often live in housing where children were encouraged. It made for a rather artificial life, but it was quiet that way.

"Hi," the girl said back, her dark eyes huge. She wore a pink shirt and a blue corduroy jumper and her feet were in little red tennis shoes. Blond curls bounced around her pretty little face. She had a look you couldn't help but smile at, and J.J. did.

"My name's J.J. What's yours?"

"Annie."

"Annie. That's a pretty name." She didn't have a lot of experience with children, and ordinarily she hardly noticed them. But something made her want to linger and talk a little more to this one. Was it her appealing face? Or the slight hint of sadness in her eyes?

"Do you live nearby?" she asked her.

Annie nodded, but she didn't leave her step.

J.J. glanced at the next condo and bit her lip. Could this be one of Jack's brood? Should she ask? For some strange reason she was hesitating, as though finding out the truth would draw her in somehow. But that was silly. Asking a question didn't imply a commitment of any kind, did it?

"Is Jack Remington your daddy?" she asked, steeling herself for the response.

Annie nodded again, and J.J. smiled again. Yes, she could see his handsome face in the lines of this little girl's bone structure.

"Well, isn't that nice?" she murmured, turning back to her door and inserting the key. Jack's daughter was awfully cute, but J.J., for one, didn't want to get to know her. The more distance she could keep between herself and the man, the better.

She'd turned the key and the door was swinging open, but before she could escape into her house, Annie's little-girl voice intruded once again.

"Do you have any babies?" she asked, her piping voice echoing through the walkway.

J.J. swung back around and stared at her. Annie had risen from her step and come a bit closer, shifting her weight from one red tennis shoe to the other. What a question to ask a complete stranger. And yet, from the look on her face, the answer seemed to be important to her.

"No," J.J. said quickly. "No, that's something I don't have."

"We have three." She held up her fingers to demonstrate the number, her expression not so much proud as matter-of-fact. "One, two, three."

"Very good," J.J. said, smiling at her. "I guess you all are lucky." Now that was a pretty disingenuous thing for her to say. Three babies sounded like a prescription for chaos to her. A netherworld filled with hellions.

She glanced at the sweet little girl standing before her and realized that hellions was possibly too strong a word. Monsters? No, you couldn't call children monsters. It wasn't right. Uncaring little beasts? From her experience, that pretty much hit the nail on the head.

But Annie nodded, her little face completely serious. She obviously agreed that babies were a good thing to have. To her it seemed perfectly normal to have a few hanging around.

"When are you going to get your baby?" she asked, her face completely solemn.

"You sound like my mother," J.J. said, laughing. "Does everyone have to have one?"

Annie frowned, not sure of the answer to that one. "We have three," she said again stoutly.

"Maybe more than your share," J.J. murmured, but not loud enough for the little girl to hear.

The bag was getting heavy and she went into the entryway and on into the kitchen, setting the bag on the counter.

Turning, she found the little girl had followed and was standing in the doorway.

"I guess you need your husband first, huh?" Annie said, continuing the conversation, merely setting things straight.

J.J. would just as soon have changed the subject. Babies and husbands were not things she'd wanted in recent years. And to tell the truth, she hadn't missed them. Suddenly everyone from her own mother to her old roommate to the little girl next door was bringing up this motherhood stuff. And though she laughed it off, as she always had, something was beginning to stick, to tickle, to bother her about it.

She began taking groceries out of the bag, putting them on the counter, and suddenly the single cans and single TV dinners seemed to be mute symbols of her lonely life. She frowned. She had to fight against such thoughts.

"You're awfully young to be thinking so much about babies," she murmured a bit defensively.

Annie took a step, bringing her farther into the kitchen.

"I have to think about babies," she said brightly. "I have to take care of them."

J.J. put the quart of milk into the refrigerator and smiled at Annie. Despite her own reservations, this seemed to be a subject that consumed the little girl. What could she do? She might as well go with it.

"You're a help at home, aren't you? Three babies." She shook her head. What a nightmare world that sounded like. "What are their names?" she asked.

"Kristi and Kathy and Baby Mack."

"Baby Mack?" She raised a questioning eyebrow.

Annie was obviously beginning to feel at home. She came all the way into the kitchen and looked around at the cabinets and the clock shaped like a large orange cat.

"We call him Baby Mack because he's soooo small," she said in her chirpy voice. "But Daddy says he has a punch like a Mack truck." Her forehead scrunched and her nose wrinkled. "What's a Mack truck?" she asked J.J. curiously.

J.J. grinned. "A big one."

"Oh." Annie turned and looked into the living room.

"How come you're living in Bambi's house?" she said out of the blue.

J.J. swung around and looked at her curiously, childhood memories of Disney films swirling. This area was awfully close to the edge of civilization, but she hardly thought wildlife came down and camped out in the houses. But then again, what did she know?

"Bambi? You mean the deer?" she asked.

Annie shook her blond curls. "No, Bambi." She said it louder, as though that might get the meaning across a little better. "She's Daddy's friend. She's pretty and she wears big high heels."

"Oh." Aha—that sort of Bambi. She suppressed a catty smile. Daddy's friend, was she? Jack had enjoyed quite a reputation as a ladies' man in the old days, but that was before marriage and kids. Surely he didn't play those games any longer.

"Well, Bambi doesn't live here anymore. I'm going to be staying here for a while."

Annie looked puzzled by that. "Where did she go?"

"I'm afraid I don't know."

"Maybe Daddy knows." She settled her chin into her palms. "She likes my Daddy."

J.J.'s head went back and something twisted in her soul. Surely good old Jack wasn't flirting around with the neighbor right under his daughter's nose?

"I'll bet a lot of women like your daddy," she murmured, looking at the girl speculatively.

Annie shrugged. "Not Marguerite. Daddy says Marguerite hates him sometimes."

J.J. knew she ought to smile pleasantly and leave this conversation lie. She tried. She really did. But in the end, curiosity got the better of integrity.

"Who... who is Marguerite?" she asked, hating herself but unable to resist.

Annie looked at her blankly. "She has orange hair. She lives with us. Her room is next to mine. She takes care of Daddy."

"Oh, she does, does she?" First Bambi, now Marguerite. She'd always pegged Jack Remington as a playboy, but this was going a bit far. For some reason, she was seething. The lousy womanizer. The profligate. The lewd and lascivious lecher. How dare he flaunt his lovers in front of this sweet little girl of his?

And what about this girl's other parent? Didn't she count in his self-centered world?

"Just...ah...where exactly is your mother?" she asked, trying to hide her real emotions.

Annie looked up and faced her with clear eyes. "My mama is in heaven," she lisped. "Daddy says God needed her."

J.J. felt as though she'd just been punched in the stomach, very hard, and her emotions made another wide swing. She felt all color drain from her face and her mouth was full of cotton. Her first impulse was to take the little girl into her arms, but that was impossible, and after the first move toward doing exactly that, she pulled back. She couldn't do it. She hardly knew her. And though the youngster was very friendly, something told her she didn't want to be hugged.

"I... I'm sure your daddy is right," she said instead.

Jack a widower—that was something she hadn't expected. It put a whole new light on things, but it was going to take her a few minutes to sort out just how. Poor man. Poor Annie. She ached inside for both of them. Hesitating, she was about to try to say something comforting, but before she got the words out, her telephone began to ring, and she swung around as though there'd been a reprieve.

"Bye," Annie said, starting toward the doorway.

"Goodbye, Annie," J.J. said on her way to the telephone. But something made her pause. The child had just told her something so horrible, she hated to see her skip off this way. "Listen," she added, hesitating. She felt as though she needed to do something for her, but she had no idea what that might be.

"I live right next door. You come on over if you need anything, okay? I'll be glad to help in any way I can."

Annie waved and disappeared out the door, and J.J. hurried back into the kitchen, reaching for the phone.

"Hello?"

The deep voice of the handsome sportscaster at the station answered. Martin Olsen had made his interest plain earlier in the day, but she wasn't in the market for a new relationship right now. She had other things on her mind and goals she was determined to reach. So after a few moments of light banter, she politely declined his invitation to dinner and rang off.

Going back to her open door, she looked out at the steps for Annie, but the girl was gone. Sighing, she closed the door and went back to the kitchen, methodically putting away the rest of the groceries. The situation with Jack and his daughter had disturbed her. She had no similar idea what the death of a wife and mother actually did to a family. She'd had no experience. But she knew it had to be horrific, and she winced, pushing away the emotions such a tragedy inspired.

It was easier to think about Jack as a playboy with all these Bambis and Marguerites and who-knows-who-elses in his life when he had these little kids to care for, and get outraged about that. But even that exasperation was fading in her. After all, what could she do about the girl? It was really none of her business if Jack wanted to run around like a teenager with brand-new hormones. Maybe that happened to widowers. Maybe they needed it.

Still, there had been such a haunted look in Annie's eyes.

Jack Remington. It was such a stroke of very bad luck to have ended up next door to the man who single-handedly had almost ruined her career before it had even begun. As she prepared a pot of lemon tea, she let her thoughts drift back to that summer ten years ago in Sacramento when she'd landed an intern job at a local television station. She'd been thrilled, even though the job had meant being handed every grubby little chore the others didn't want to be bothered with. That was the way it was when you were low man on the totem pole, and she had been glad to put up with it for the experience and the pleasure of being in the business she adored.

She'd spent the summer taking in every bit of knowledge she could glean. She'd watched Jack from afar. He'd been the star anchor at the station at the time, and everyone had treated him like a king. She'd been ecstatic when he smiled at her, but he'd only spoken to her once.

It was late in the summer and she'd finally had a chance to go on camera with a newsbreak at the hour. She'd given it everything she had and most people had been generous with their praise. And then Jack had come sauntering along and looked her up and down, and she'd held her breath, waiting to hear what he had to say.

"You're a very pretty girl," he said at last. "I'll bet you were a cheerleader in high school, weren't you?"

Thinking he meant it as a compliment, she'd colored and smiled at him. "Why, yes, I was."

His mouth had twitched at the corners. "That's what I thought," he said, the scorn plain in his tone. "Well, let me give you a little bit of advice, Miss Jenkins. Pay a little more attention to the program your newsbreak is interrupting. In the movie playing tonight, a child has just been told he might never walk again. The viewers are crying their eyes out. And then you come on, grinning like a loon and shouting out the news item as though it were the main cheer at a pep rally." He shook his head. "You're going to have to do better than that, Miss Jenkins, if you think you're going to get anywhere in this business."

He'd walked away, leaving her behind in a humiliated heap. Not only had he hated her style, he hadn't remembered her name right. No one met her eyes for the rest of the day, and the next morning she was told her services were no longer needed at the station.

The shock of finding herself sidelined so quickly still stung. Okay, so he had been right, she'd been so anxious about her spot she hadn't thought to put it into context. She'd learned a lot from what he'd told her, she had to admit that. But still—he didn't need to lecture her so harshly in front of the entire staff, and most of all, he shouldn't have had her fired. It just wasn't right and she resented it to this day.

The night before, after their meeting around her hot tub, she'd scanned the local listing, looking to see what station he was working for these days, but she hadn't been able to find any mention of his name, and that had surprised her.

This morning at work, she'd brought him up to Martin, the sportscaster.

"I didn't know Jack Remington was working here in St. Johns," she'd said, making her voice as casual as she could.

"Jack Remington?" Martin's handsome brow had furled. "Who's Jack Remington?"

But another employee standing nearby had heard of him. "Jack Remington? You're kidding. Where did you see him?"

She hesitated, and something about his interest made her wary. "Uh, I thought I saw him near the condo complex where I'm staying. Maybe I was wrong."

"Jack Remington," the man had mused, thinking back. "He used to be the best, you know. He was slated for major network success when he dropped out of sight. I wonder whatever happened to him."

"Yes," J.J. had murmured, moving away. "I wonder."

So it seemed he had forsaken his old career. Strange. Still, she would rather not ever find out why than to have to deal with him again. And since she was only slated for the area for a few weeks, she doubted that would be a problem.

She picked up the invitation to her friend's baby shower and smiled at the silly duckling with a bow, but her smile faded as she read the date again. It was only weeks away. She didn't think she was going to be able to make it. After all these years, it would be wonderful to see the old gang again. Pinning the invitation to the kitchen bulletin board, she resolved to see if she could find a way to go.

She went back to the station at three, and it was evening before she returned home again, a sack from the local fried chicken outlet under her arm. As she came up the walk, she thought she heard animals in the trees, but when she cocked her head and listened, she realized it was babies crying. A lot of babies crying.

She frowned. She had only one thin wall between her condo and Jack's. Letting herself into her place, she found her unease had been warranted. The crying sounded even louder in her living room than it had outside.

"What on earth is going on in there?" she muttered irritably. "It sounds like a baby convention."

A soft knocking on her door got her attention and she opened it to find Annie standing there, her lower lip quivering and moisture welling in her eyes.

"Annie!" she cried, pulling the child into her entryway. "What is it? What's the matter?"

The little girl burst into tears, but she tried to force back the flow, wincing away when J.J. tried to comfort her with a hug. J.J. drew back, uncertain of how to deal with this. She wasn't used to children, hadn't been around them since she'd been a child herself. Annie looked so sad, so pathetic, she wanted badly to do something for her. But what?

Her first instinct was that something terrible had happened, but that thought was beginning to recede, despite the child's inability to get her story out. Inexperienced as she was with children, she had a feeling no one was lying bleeding somewhere. This had all the earmarks of a problem dealing with the emotions, not with physical danger. Some of her adrenaline slowed a bit, and she risked touching the little girl's hair.

"Just take it easy," she murmured, frowning at her worriedly.

Meanwhile, the tears Annie was trying to hold back kept squeezing out. "I...I..." Her face crumpled and she couldn't get the words out.

J.J. turned and grabbed a tissue from a box on the counter and handed it to her, bending close, aching to help but not knowing how.

"Just take a deep breath and tell me slowly," she encouraged her.

Annie tried, but the sobs were shaking her and it took a few minutes before she could speak.

"It's all my fault," she wailed, hiccuping.

"What's your fault, Annie?" J.J. coaxed, stroking her hair and not receiving a rebuff.

"M-M-Marguerite," Annie forced out. "She's gone."

"Gone?" Marguerite? Wasn't that the live-in girlfriend, the floozy? Of course, she had no hard evidence, but things Annie had said that very afternoon had pointed in the direction of *painted lady*. And if that was the case, good riddance to her. Little girls like Annie needed...well, she wasn't sure what they needed. J.J. went down on her knees to get closer to the sad little face.

"Oh, honey, how could that possibly be your fault?"

She rubbed her eyes with both fists. "I...I didn't like the pot roast."

J.J. blinked. "The pot roast." There had to be a connection here. If only she could see what it was.

Annie nodded, finally getting everything but her lower lip under control. "I couldn't eat it. I just couldn't."

"Oh." The picture was clearing. "Did Marguerite make the pot roast?" she guessed.

Annie nodded again. "I hate it." She made a face, shuddering. "It's yucky." She looked up at J.J. earnestly, intent upon explaining. "It's got like hairy things and then the big globs of jiggly fat stuff and when it gets in your mouth it—"

"I see. I understand." J.J. cut her off hurriedly, suppressing a smile, and stroked the little girl's hair again, her fingers catching in the curls. "And she's touchy about food critics, is she?"

"Uh-huh." Annie nodded vigorously. "She put all her clothes in a bag and she went out the door."

"Ah."

"And it's all my fault."

"Oh, honey." A thought occurred to her and she looked at the girl sharply. "Did your daddy tell you that?"

Annie blinked at her, not understanding the question. "Huh?"

J.J.'s entire opinion of the man hung in the balance. She spoke again, making the words very clear, and watched for the tiniest reaction.

"Did your daddy say it was your fault?"

She shook her head, and her curls, damp from her copious tears, tried to give their usual bounce.

"Daddy said, 'Oh, never mind. We can take care of things without her.'"

"Oh." Well, there went that theory. At least Jack wasn't an ogre to his child. She wasn't sure if she was relieved or disappointed.

"Then the babies started to cry. They won't stop. And Daddy said, 'Go get Mrs. Lark to help, quick.' I said, 'Okay, Daddy,' and I went really, really quick. I knocked on Mrs. Lark's door. I knocked really, really loud, but she didn't come out. And I knocked on Mr. Gomez's door, but he wasn't home. So I came here."

"Your daddy needs help, does he?" Startled, she looked toward the still open doorway. "Is it just the crying? Or does he need a doctor? Or the police?" She realized it might be best to make things clear.

"Uh-uh." She shook her head so that her curls hit her in the nose. "He needs help with the babies. 'Cuz they keep crying."

"Oh." She hesitated. That sort of help was supposed to be within the realm of 'women's work', wasn't it? Which meant she ought to be able to handle it. But she didn't want to do this. She really didn't want to see Jack again if she could help it and she was hoping for an excuse not to go.

"What exactly is wrong with the babies?"

Annie's wide brown eyes stared at her. "They're crying."

J.J. narrowly averted rolling her eyes. That fact had pretty much been established. But did babies just cry? Wasn't there a reason? She hesitated. "Yes, I know that," she said at last. "In fact, I knew that before you got here."

Annie was surprised and somewhat captivated. "You did?"

"Sure. Listen. You can hear them through the walls."

She led her into the living room and took her to the wall, placing her hand against the surface, so she could feel as well as hear. Annie listened and her face brightened.

"I hear them!" she cried. Then a cloud came over her expression once again. "They're getting too loud. Come on." Annie took J.J.'s hand and tugged, looking up at her anxiously. "Come on. Hurry."

J.J. managed to keep the groan inside and she followed reluctantly. But she went. And she steeled herself, preparing, against all common sense, to walk right into the lion's den.

Three

The entryway was almost a duplicate of the one for the condo where J.J. was staying, but the rest of the house looked very different. Where her place was starkly dramatic, with chrome and glass and dark polished wood, Jack's was light and airy—and soft. The couches were overstuffed and the chairs were plump with pillows. The colors were pastels and the carpeting was as thick as winter fur. No angles—everything looked rounded at the edges.

It's a cartoon house, she thought to herself as she entered. *But the sound track's all wrong.*

The sound track, in fact, was very loud. Not only were the babies howling at the top of their lungs, but Jack was singing at the top of his. She caught sight of him as she rounded the corner into the family room, and what she saw left her gaping. This was hardly the picture of the debonair sophisticate she remembered.

One baby sat on a fluffy blue blanket on the floor, her face red from crying. Another, smaller child was lying on his back and screaming at the ceiling, his arms and legs whirling like propellers. And between them, in a padded rocking chair, sat Jack, a third baby propped against his shoulder, rocking furiously and singing for all he was worth.

The song was some country tune about wives who took their love to town. J.J. was knocked out, speechless. She would have figured him as an Edith Piaf fan, or maybe Billie Holiday—something genteel and just a bit jaded, but always classy. And here he was, singing with a twang.

He caught sight of her, but that didn't stop him. In fact, she could have sworn he only got louder, rocking and patting the baby on his shoulder in time to the music, his blue eyes daring her to laugh at him.

She pulled her gaze away from that amazing sight and looked from one squalling baby to the other with growing horror, then noticed that Annie was looking up into her face as though she expected something that wasn't happening.

"Annie," she said, shrugging helplessly, "I don't know much about babies. What should I do?"

"You pick 'em up," Annie told her wisely, shouting to be heard over the din. "Look."

And she dipped down and scooped one baby, expertly swinging the child up against her shoulder. The move took a major effort, however, as the baby wasn't much smaller than Annie herself, and she staggered under the weight. J.J. helped her to the couch, then turned and looked down at the last lonely weeper.

The baby was sitting on the floor, tears running down her fat little cheeks. She wore yellow pajamas and a pink bib with "Kristi" embroidered on it. J.J. gazed at her nervously and flexed her fingers, wondering exactly how she was going to do this.

Just swing her up, she told herself silently. *It looks so easy.*

She took a step toward the child and the baby stopped crying, staring at her, little round eyes huge and wary.

"Hi," J.J. said cheerfully, holding out her hand the way she might approach a strange dog. "Hi, Kristi."

Kristi stared up at her for a long, long moment, and then her face crumpled again, eyes squeezed tightly shut, mouth wide and howling. Startled, J.J. pulled back and looked at Jack.

Mercifully, his song had come to an end and he was mainly humming now. He interrupted that long enough to call out, "He who hesitates is lost. Go for it."

And suddenly she realized he was talking to her. She looked at the crying baby, and then back at Jack again, completely lost. "But I . . ."

"Oh, come on. She doesn't bite." He glanced over the top of his now quietly sobbing baby to ask Annie, "She hasn't bitten anyone yet, has she?"

Annie shook her head firmly. "She only has one tooth," she said sensibly.

Jack shrugged, his eyes twinkling. "There, you see? We're loud, but we're basically civilized around here. Go on. Pick her up."

J.J. took a deep breath. Reaching down, she practically closed her eyes as she took hold of the child, but a few seconds later, Kristi was in her arms and she held her awkwardly. Jack rose, carrying his little bundle gently and nodded toward the rocking chair.

"Go ahead and sit there," he said. "They love it." And he left the room.

J.J. hesitated, but there wasn't much choice. Kristi was yelling too hard to do much else with. Sitting gingerly and shifting the baby, trying to position her up against her shoulder the way she'd seen the others do, she held her breath as she tried to settle the child, but the crying seemed to be increasing in intensity, and though the baby didn't struggle, she was weeping as though the world had turned against her and her heart was about to break.

J.J. looked over at Annie, feeling definitely inadequate. Annie's baby was quieting, snuggling against her and winding down to a whimper.

"Good boy, Baby Mack," Annie said. "Good boy." She gave him a pleased pat and looked up at J.J. "Kristi likes to cry," she noted. "Daddy says she's the champion crier in the family."

Oh, great. They gave her the most difficult one right off the bat? She started patting and rocking and praying under her breath, but without much hope. Surely she was doomed to spend the night rocking with a baby howling in her ear. That just seemed to be the way things were going to fall.

But as she rocked, a strange thing began to happen. The little body that had felt so stiff and awkward began to relax. The round head stopped bobbing against her shoulder and pressed into the hollow of her neck. One little fist grabbed hold of the collar of her shirt. And the crying began to slow.

And another funny thing happened at the same time. When she'd first picked the baby up, she'd almost wrinkled her nose, sure the child would be sticky and smelly. And at first, the rejection she'd felt from the baby had made her think she was right. But now... well, now, with Kristi snuggling against her and only whimpering, and slowly falling asleep, a whole new sense of her came over J.J.

Now she was soft and sweet and delicious to hold, like nothing she'd ever held before.

Funny. Very funny.

Looking around the room, she noticed that Annie seemed to have taken the one they called Baby Mack off to bed. Jack came back into the room and she looked at him warily, but his smile was pleased, if quirky.

"Well, you did it—is it Miss Jensen?" he said, taking the baby from her and slinging her effortlessly against his shoulder with the practiced ease of a longtime daddy.

"J.J.," she said, moving to the edge of her seat and watching him, impressed, if a bit confused. This scene hardly fit the picture she'd had of Jack all these years, and certainly seemed at odds with her more recent vision of him as a playboy.

"Ah yes, J.J." Kristi had settled down immediately in those familiar arms, her eyelids heavy and falling over her bright blue eyes. She was worn-out from all that crying and ready to rest up for her next round. He patted her rhythmically and swayed to the beat, turning to smile at J.J. again.

"Well, you need some refreshment, I can see that."

"That's all right." She jumped up like a startled deer, ready to make her escape. "I'll just be going now."

"Oh, no, you don't. You don't get off that easily."

He said it with such authority, she found herself sinking back into the chair again as though she'd been programmed into doing what he said, as though he were still the boss.

"You need a cup of tea," he said cheerfully, starting toward the bedroom with his bundle. "And I'm brewing a pot right now. You just sit right there and relax. I'll be back." He dropped a kiss on his baby's fuzzy head. "Come on, angel face," he crooned to her. "Let's get you to bed."

Sitting back, she watched him go, feeling torn. She thought of her bag of fast-food chicken sitting on the counter in her own condo drying up, and she thought of her early call for the morning show, but she had to admit there was something about this beautiful man that drew her in. She wanted to stay for a few minutes, just to see what made this guy tick.

Annie came out of the bedroom and gazed at her. "I have new shoes," she told her seriously. "Black ones. I'm going to wear them to church on Sunday."

"Lucky girl." J.J. smiled at her, noting again how similar her facial structure was to her father's. "I love new shoes."

Annie nodded, and Jack came out, dropping to sit on the couch with a sigh of weary relief. "They're all asleep, at least for now," he said.

"Can I have juice?" Annie asked.

"Oh, sure, honey," he said absently, "But say 'may I?'" he added as she left for the kitchen. Turning, he gave J.J. a warm, encompassing smile that made shivers start down her backbone, reminding her to keep her guard up. The man was too attractive for his own good—and for hers. She had to be careful not to fall under his spell.

"You're a lifesaver, J.J.," he said easily. "J.J.," he repeated. "What are the initials for?"

"My name," she replied shortly.

"Ah, it's a secret." He grinned as though that only made her more enchanting. "Can anybody guess?"

She raised an eyebrow. Why on earth did he deem it necessary to turn the old charm on her, of all people? "You can guess all you like," she said, her tone almost defensive.

"A lady of mystery." He looked at her speculatively as Annie came out of the kitchen with a plastic tumbler of juice in her hands.

"It isn't Jennifer Jones, by any chance? Or are you too young to remember who she is?"

"I've seen a few old movies in my time. And no, it isn't Jennifer Jones."

"Julie Junie?" asked Annie, getting in on the act. "Janie Jamas?"

Jack threw his head back and laughed. "Never mind, pumpkin," he told his serious little daughter. "J.J. wants to be called by those initials, and that is what we shall call her. It's none of our business why she wants to keep her name a secret."

J.J. opened her mouth to protest, then closed it again. He was teasing her and she knew it. Enough. She wasn't going to get sucked into his games.

"Well, you seem to have your hands full with all these children," she noted, trying to change the subject.

He nodded. "That we do. It must seem a madhouse to you. But things will get back to normal around here soon enough."

"If Marguerite comes back," Annie muttered tragically.

There was an awkward pause, and then Jack filled it with a quick laugh.

"Marguerite," he said scornfully. "Let her go, I say. We'll find someone better than Marguerite." He turned and looked with interest at J.J., as though he'd suddenly had a bright idea. "Can you cook?"

J.J. didn't get a chance to answer. The telephone rang and Jack went to take the call while she stayed behind, fuming. Could she cook! What a question.

She began glancing at the door, wondering how she could get out without that long-promised cup of tea, when he returned to the room and said breezily, "The tea should be just about ready. I'll get us some. You sit tight." And he went on into the kitchen.

J.J. looked at Annie. Annie looked back. J.J. tried to think of something to say. What did one talk to a five-year-old about? Luckily Annie knew.

"I can dance," she told her. "Wanna see?"

"Of course." She smiled at the little girl. "I'd love to see."

Rising from her chair, Annie twirled and twirled, her arms out, until she fell into a dizzy heap at J.J.'s feet. J.J. looked down at her, worried, but Jack called out, "Get up, pumpkin. You're in the way of the tea party," as he came into the room, hardly wasting a glance at his collapsed daughter, and Annie got up quickly enough, sitting in her chair to await her cup of tea.

Jack poured and passed the cups. Annie's was mostly milk. J.J. took hers without sugar, so she was easy. But she watched this big man performing these housewifely chores and marveled. What had happened to him to make him so domestic? That certainly wasn't the way she remembered him.

They chatted inconsequentially for a moment, sipping their tea, and J.J. had to admit it had a soothing effect. She had only been in the maelstrom for half an hour and she felt wrung out like an old dishrag. Jack and Annie had been in it all day. How did they manage?

Annie disappeared into the kitchen and Jack told J.J. about something cute Baby Mack had done earlier in the day, making her laugh, then about something funny Annie had said.

"How old is she?" J.J. asked, smiling.

"Five and a half," he said with pride.

"She seems so...so wise, so articulate."

"Oh yes." His gaze seemed to darken. "Annie's been through a lot. Her mother died soon after the triplets were born. And ever since, she's had to do a lot more than any five-year-old should have to." His voice grew husky. "She's my gem."

Unaccountably J.J. felt tears stinging her eyes, and she blinked them back in horror. Damn the man! He could play her like a fine violin. He seemed to know where every emotion was located and how to exploit it. She should go home.

"And what is it that you do, J.J.?" Jack asked, studying her, before she had a chance to excuse herself.

She hesitated. She didn't really want to tell him the business she was involved in. She was afraid that might make him wary in some way. She had a feeling he didn't want his old world to know where he was or what he was doing. She wasn't sure why she felt that, but she did.

Something crashed in the kitchen and he rose quickly, automatically following the sounds of disaster as though it were something he did all the time. And she supposed it was. She'd never seen a more hands-on daddy in her life.

Sitting back, she gazed around the room. Toys and blankets were strewn on chairs and under tables, and stacks of clean diapers sat beside picture books and baby games. She didn't think she'd ever been in a house so geared toward young people. Pictures dominated the decorating motif— pictures of Annie at various stages, pictures of the triplets.

She couldn't find one of Jack, nor of any woman who might be the mother of this brood. Annie's words came back to her—"My mother is in heaven." You would think he would have pictures of her everywhere. She frowned. Come to think of it, you would think he would have a sadder look. Funny.

Suddenly another encounter she'd had with Jack came to mind, something she hadn't thought about in years. There had once come a time when she'd gone in to see Jack Remington. A week or so after she'd been let go—terminated, released, fired, laid off, and all those other ugly words—

she'd been in a state bordering on depression. She'd tried every other station in town with no luck, and she'd begun having paranoid thoughts that Jack might have blackballed her. It looked as though her chances of being in the business, which had once looked so good, were fading away.

Gathering all her strength and all her courage, she'd made her way downtown and into the station, her speech of outrage and her request for mercy all nicely memorized and rehearsed, over and over again. She was ready to go to battle with the big man.

She'd bypassed the receptionist and headed straight for his office, surprised to find the door propped open and a small knot of people standing out in the hallway, watching what was going on inside. Lights had been set up, and someone with a video camera was calling out orders.

"What's going on?" she asked someone at the scene.

"New promo for the news hour," a secretary told her. "Jack is not enjoying this," she added with a giggle.

And it seemed she was right. J.J. got closer and looked in. Jack's face had a rebellious look.

"Just a few more, Jack," Gloria Barker was saying. Executive producer of the evening news hour, she always had a slightly anxious look, as though she'd just seen the ratings and they were dropping. "This will only take another moment or so."

The cameraman swung his camera around and announced in a voice loud enough to hear in nearby homes, "Since you're the heartthrob of the station, we should get a shot of you mesmerizing a lady or two, don't you think?"

Jack's brow darkened and his full lower lip came out. "No, I don't think. It's not part of the job."

Jack's annoyance was plain on his face and J.J. sighed and fidgeted. This was not going to be a good time to approach him.

The cameraman said something else and Jack's frown deepened. "What do you want, a seduction pose?" Jack looked incredulous. "I don't think so."

The cameraman spoke again. Though J.J. couldn't make out his words, Jack's answer was clear. He spun and demanded of Gloria Barker, "Is there anything in my contract that says I have to do this? If so, I want a renegotiation."

"Jack . . . please." She put a hand on his arm and looked up at him pleadingly. "Do this. Do it for me. It's so important. You know the station's in serious trouble. If we can't bring up the ratings . . ."

He took a deep breath, obviously trying hard to keep his temper. His eyes seemed to glitter. "I'm a newsman, not a movie star."

"I know that, but . . . Jack. I need you to do this. Just this once. Please?"

She looked up at him like an orphan in the snow, and he groaned, melting.

"All right, Gloria. For you." He signaled the man with the photo equipment. "Fine. You want a seduction, you'll have one. Get me a woman and let's get this over with."

"Yes!" the cameraman said, pumping his arm and turning to give the small crowd a quick survey.

"How about you? Would you like to be in the picture?"

J.J. turned to look behind her, wondering whom he was calling to.

"You," he said, pointing at her. "Come on in here."

"Me?" At first, his intention really didn't penetrate. She was still wondering how she was going to get in to see Jack with all these people around, and how he was going to react after all this hassle, and suddenly she was being pushed and pulled into his office and someone was coming at her with a large powder puff and an eyebrow pencil. "What? Wait!"

"No time to wait. Come on."

They tugged at her clothes and adjusted her makeup and presented her, ready to go, to Jack, who was brewing a very dark storm in his eyes.

"Are we ready?" he snapped. "Let's get this show on the road."

"Okay," said the camera guy. "Let the wooing begin."

Jack finally looked at her for the first time, and as she remembered it, he hesitated. He'd recognized her, but there was something else in his eyes, and whether or not it had anything to do with his having had her fired, she was never sure.

"You know..." he began. He looked down into her face and then he turned away as though there were something about her that disturbed him. But the others waved him back and he returned, shrugging.

Meanwhile, J.J. found it impossible to do anything but stand there with her mouth open, flabbergasted. How had this happened? She was about to be seduced on camera by Jack Remington. A few weeks before, this might have been the answer to a dream. But now... didn't they understand? Didn't anyone remember? The man had just had her fired last week!

"Take your places. Jack, put your hand on her shoulder and lean over her... good, that's the way."

She felt as though she were moving in a misty fantasy. It was completely unreal. His face hovered over hers, his lips almost touching her, but not quite. She held her breath, overwhelmed by his closeness, feeling faint, feeling a swoon coming on—and then she heard him swear under his breath and she realized he was gritting his teeth.

"Enough?" he called out, still holding her in that impossible position.

"No, wait a minute. We need a little more passion, Jack. And move to the left a little. The light wasn't set up right. Try this."

The crew went on and on, posing them in every imaginable combination. His anger was growing and it was beginning to show through. But she was moving in a dream, as though she couldn't do anything else, as though she had no will of her own. She was involved, but somehow she was also a fly on the wall, watching this as if from afar. She was participant and observer, all at the same time, and for the moment, nothing seemed real.

Nothing, that is, except Jack. He was so close, she could sense his breath on her neck, feel his body heat through his shirt where her hand rested on his chest, breathe in the scent of his after-shave. His handsome maleness was intoxicating. And his annoyance with the whole thing was palpable.

Finally he had had enough. Grabbing her by the shoulders, he pulled her toward him.

"This is the last shot," he said, the finality of his decision clear in his tone. "You want passion? I'll give you passion. But this is it."

She was too far gone in the whole ridiculous situation to stop things now. She didn't try to stop, she didn't try to think. She just raised her face and closed her eyes, and he kissed her.

His kiss had it all—waves crashing on the beach and angels singing in the sky and the scent of roses in the air. Who could ask for anything more?

And at the same time, it wasn't real and she knew it. It was as phony as the passion he was pretending to feel. And as soon as it was over, he drew back crisply and said, "Thank you very much, Miss . . . Jennings, is it? I'm really very sorry. Sometimes this business . . ."

He let the sentence dangle there, turning away from her, leaving the office for the broadcasting booth. She watched him go, still stunned. And then she went home and never tried to contact him again.

But the entire episode stayed with her for months. She went back to school and had no other problems getting jobs, but Jack and his kiss troubled her for a long, long time. The infuriating thing was, she knew he hadn't given it another thought since.

Well, that was just fine. Memories were the last things she wanted to revive. She thought of that entire scene in his office now, and she cringed, embarrassed by it and glad he didn't seem to remember it at all. She'd been young, she'd been vulnerable. She wasn't like that anymore. Ten years in the business had hardened her in many ways. She didn't let a pretty face bowl her over any longer. Too many pretty faces were mere masks to evil people.

Not that she thought Jack was evil, she corrected herself quickly. No, far from it, despite the problems he may have given her in the past. No man could take care of babies the way he did and harbor ill toward the world. He was just— self-centered, egotistical, arrogant. Things like that. In other words, a typical man.

He and Annie returned from the kitchen with tales of a major cleanup needed after Annie dropped the jug of juice. J.J. listened and laughed and plotted her retreat. She had to go. She couldn't stay and let Jack attempt to charm her this way. She'd enjoyed despising him all these years and she hated to give it up, but she certainly wasn't going to let herself go to the opposite extreme. Not on such short notice, at any rate.

She began to gather herself together. "Well, thank you very much for the tea, but I'm going to have to get going," she ventured.

Jack turned and fixed her with a penetrating stare. "Just a minute, J.J.," he said quietly. "I want to talk to you about something."

She felt her heart quicken. Did he remember, then? Had it all come back to him at last? Was he planning to apologize? Darn. That was the last thing she wanted.

"I really need to get home," she protested weakly, looking toward the door as a way to avoid looking into his eyes.

"Of course. But J.J., you can see that we are in need here. The fact is, I'd like to hire you."

"What?" Her head swung around and she stared up into his deep blue eyes. He couldn't have said what she thought she'd heard. Surely not.

He smiled. "I'd like to hire you to take Marguerite's place."

"What?" Outrage poured through her and she jumped up from her chair. Marguerite's place? As far as she knew, Marguerite was a live-in honey who did some child-care things on the side. What did he think she looked like? Was the man insane?

No, this was too much. He actually thought a few moments of charm and a cup of tea would bowl her right over, didn't he? This wasn't like the old days, when a word from him could practically change the course of her life.

"I don't think so," she said crisply, one hand on her hip, her chin in the air. "It's not exactly my line of work."

Jack looked surprised. "Are you already working for someone?" His shrug was very continental, very man-of-the-world. All things could be remedied, all things could be explained. "Tell me what he pays you. I'll double it."

Her jaw dropped. "You . . . !" She couldn't think of anything bad enough that she could say in front of the child. "Forget it," she demanded, turning on her heel and striding for the exit.

"J.J." He came after her and helped her with the door. "I hope you'll reconsider. You would be perfect for what I need."

She felt her face turning bright red and she turned to give him what for—but when she did, her gaze met his and something scary happened. It came from out of nowhere and struck like a lightning bolt. He stared at her and she looked back into his intensely blue eyes, and for a long moment, she felt as though she could dive right into all that blueness and drown. She didn't think, didn't breathe. The room was spinning, and she remembered with sudden power what it had been like to kiss that full, hard mouth of his. A tremor started deep in her soul, and she couldn't look away. It was as though an electric current passed between them, making her jump, making him jerk his head back. For just a moment, for a fragile second, she clung to the hope that she was imagining things.

But no. He'd felt it, too. She could see it on his face, in the look of surprise in his eyes.

"Damn, damn, damn," she muttered, shaking her head and frowning at him furiously when she finally regained control of her senses.

"No thanks, Jack Remington," she added with more force, trying desperately to maintain a little dignity. "I have my own needs, and they have nothing to do with you."

Turning on her heel, she hurried from the doorway without saying another word. When she got into her own place, she closed the door and locked it, breathing hard.

The nerve of the man. Take Marguerite's place, indeed!

She would sooner get a job as an alligator trainer.

Ha!

Four

___

Yoga positions. J.J. hadn't done yoga for years, but she needed them this morning. She needed to focus her mind and block out the man next door, and there was nothing like sitting in the lotus position with every muscle screaming bloody murder, humming a little chant and staring into nothing, to settle you down and calm the senses. In recent years she'd been caught up in aerobic dancing and cross-country ski machines, but today she was back into yoga.

She ended her session with a wobbly headstand and got back onto her feet and staggered to the kitchen for a glass of orange juice.

"My, I feel a lot better now," she lied to herself, forcing a bright smile on her face. If you made yourself smile, you got happier. She really believed that. She lived it.

Going on into the bedroom to change for work, she made a resolution. She was going to forget about Jack Remington and his wild brood. She was here to work, to make herself known to the powers in charge in New York, to further her career. She was not here to listen to propositions from men who'd fired her, or to nursemaid little babies. If she'd wanted babies, she would have married old what-was-his-name—Barry Newman. He'd been her agent in Sacramento a number of years ago and he'd been crazy about her, bent on settling down and starting a ranch someplace.

But she'd had her eye on the prize. She'd always been that way. She'd never regretted turning Barry down. Of course, it might have been harder to do if she'd actually been in love with him. Love was another one of those little luxuries she hadn't allowed herself since high school.

She'd learned early that life was hard, that you had to work for what you wanted out of it. She watched friends fall by the wayside, hung up on love and walking around pregnant with little ones hanging on them, their dreams like dust in the wind. She didn't have time for things like love. She had to hurry, to work a little harder, to make it up to that next rung on the ladder. She didn't dare look down. If she did, she knew she'd fall.

And she knew what it was like when you fell. She'd grown up that way. Her father had gone out with his buddies one Friday night and never come back. Her mother had worked as a practical nurse in a rest home. J.J. and her brothers had cooked and cleaned and kept the house from the time they were in elementary school, and as soon as they turned sixteen, they each had jobs, as well. Someone had to put food on the table. When J.J. had been awarded the scholarship to go to college, her mother had been horrified at the waste of it all. Why should she go off and have fun for four years while the rest of them were left behind, trying hard to make it from one paycheck to the next? She quickly informed J.J. not to expect any pocket money coming her way. They couldn't afford it.

J.J. had never expected her mother to help support her. She'd gone off to college because she'd known it was her only hope to end up with a better life than her mother had had. She'd worked in the dining hall for her room and board, and then taken a part-time job at a local pizza place, as well, and still kept her high academic average. Yes, she knew what it was like to pinch pennies, and she was bound and determined she would never have to live that way again.

One more sip of orange juice and she would be off to the station.

If only the telephone hadn't rung. If only she had kept her resolve and walked on out that door without answering it. But she hesitated, wondering if it might be the station telling her not to come in, or to pick up doughnuts on the way, or any number of things. After all, who else had her number?

So she picked it up.

"Hello?" she said, reaching for her coat.

"J.J.?" said a deep, rich voice, and her heart sank.

Jack Remington. How could it be that he was calling her after what he'd offered her the night before, after the way she'd turned him down in no uncertain terms? She rolled her eyes and swallowed hard, settling herself.

"Yes, this is J.J.," she said coolly. "How did you get this number?"

"The number never changes over there," he said smoothly. "It comes with the place. As I told you before, the tenant who lived there until recently was a good friend."

Ah yes, the inimitable Bambi.

"Listen, Jack," she began. "I was just on my way out—"

"I hate to do this," he interrupted. "But I'm in a bind. I need your help."

She felt her insides quiver. Jack Remington needed her help, and her feminine soul responded just as most feminine souls would do—yearning to do anything in her power to help him. But her mind was stronger. And her mind was going to win this time.

"I'm really very sorry, Jack," she said, feeling as though a stiff wind were at her back, helping her along. "But I'm going to be late if I don't—"

"Here's the problem," he broke in once again. "Annie has to get to kindergarten. I usually put the triplets in a three-seat stroller and walk her over, but it's drizzling this morning, and Kristi has a sniffle. Could you possibly run Annie over? It's only two blocks away."

The wind vanished, leaving her sails slack and lifeless. "When does she have to go?" she asked in a choked voice.

"In about ten minutes."

What could she say? How could she be so churlish as to deny the child a ride to kindergarten? Besides, she liked Annie. The poor girl couldn't help it that she had a cad for a father. Taking a deep breath, she squared her shoulders and prepared to do her duty.

"All right," she said crisply. "I'll be over in a few minutes."

She hung up quickly, avoiding a chat. Now she had ten minutes to build up a major case of nerves over seeing him again. Darn it. Where were those doughnuts when you really needed them?

Jack hung up the telephone and called into Annie's room. "It's okay. J.J.'s going to give you a ride."

His daughter came out of the bedroom dressed for school. He watched her emerge, her little feet in tiny saddle shoes, her plaid jumper slightly askew, her hair nicely combed in front and tangled in back, and his heart was full—full of love, full of regret.

"Come here, rascal," he said huskily, picking up a hairbrush and attacking the tangle. "You learn a lot at school today, okay? Forget all about me and the triplets for a few hours. Just be a kid."

"Okay, Daddy," she said solemnly. "Did Marguerite call yet?"

He hesitated. "Honey, I don't think Marguerite is coming back this time. I called the agency about getting a new housekeeper. They're going to call me back today."

He watched her face, but there was no visible reaction.

"Okay," she said, and set off for the kitchen where she knew he'd prepared a bowl of cereal for her.

He watched her go for a moment, then turned back into her room to get her coat. She had a picture of her mother by her bedside, a large, glossy portrait that showed a beautiful woman. It wasn't his favorite picture. In fact, he hated it. The picture showed her beauty, but it showed hints of the rest, as well, especially around the eyes—the wildness, the selfish streak. But for some reason Annie loved it, so here it sat. He hardly ever let himself look at it, but this time he caught sight of it and stood as though it had caught him, somehow. He stared at it, clutching the little coat but thinking about a long-ago place and a long-ago love. Emotion was welling up in him, choking his throat, and he swore softly as he finally turned away.

What the hell was wrong with him this morning? He was losing it over everything. Maybe he'd been playing mom for so long, he was developing female hormones.

The doorbell rang and he went to let J.J. in. Opening the door to her pretty, wary face made him smile. What a contrast she was to what he was used to. He wished, fleetingly, that she'd agreed to come and work for them. With her around, there would be more smiles. He could feel it.

"Hi," he said, throwing open the door. "I really appreciate this. Annie's just finishing her breakfast. She'll be out in a second."

"Okay." J.J. stepped in tentatively, glancing at her watch. She was bound and determined to keep this on a professional and very formal level. And to do that, she was going to have to avoid looking into his eyes. There could be no repetition of what had happened the night before.

"Will Annie need to be picked up, too?"

He thought for a moment. "Well, if the rain stops..."

"What time?" J.J. asked, cutting to the chase, as she tugged on the cuff of her blouse and straightened her jacket.

"Twelve-thirty," he said, a crooked grin twisting his face as he looked her over. He could see right through her motivations, and her apprehension amused him.

He'd felt the current that had sizzled between them the night before, but he wasn't going to take it seriously. After all, she was a very attractive woman, and he'd been lonely a long, long time. It was only natural, and certainly didn't have to be acted upon. He could take in her almond-shaped dark eyes with the riff of bangs that hung right over them like a teasing curtain and feel his insides begin to tighten, and enjoy the sensation without having to grab her and head for the nearest bed. Although the thought was tempting.

He leashed his grin and told her simply, "Thanks."

She nodded, trying to avoid looking at him. He was so big and good-looking and his gaze always had that knowing look, as though he could read her mind. She hated that. Feeling restless, she glanced at her watch again.

He noticed the gesture, and noticed how she was dressed, as well. A trim and expensive-looking wool suit with a silk scarf tied artistically at her neckline made her look very professional. She had on a lot of makeup, as well, and that was a familiar sight to him, though it was a stark contrast to the way she'd looked the night before. It was the style used at television stations when one was expected to go on camera. He gazed at her with a slight frown.

"I guess you really do have a job," he murmured, looking her over, speaking his thoughts without censoring them first.

She reacted with a flush, which was getting to be a habit around him.

"Yes, of course I have a job," she said somewhat defensively, reaching up reflexively to straighten her scarf.

He raised an eyebrow. "I thought…" But his voice trailed off and he bit back what he was about to say. Sometimes, he reminded himself, he said too much and said it too honestly. People, especially women, seemed to take offense.

She was flushing even more furiously, afraid she had a clue as to what he had been getting at. She'd known it from the first, from the way he looked at her the afternoon at the hot tub, the way he'd grinned at her the night before.

"What did you think?" she demanded, determined to put this suspicion to rest with a dose of truth. Get things out in the open and you could deal with them. Left unsaid, they tended to fester.

"Nothing." He shook his head, but the frown was back as though he were puzzling things out. "This means you must work at the station."

"Why would you have thought anything else?" she asked tartly, though she had a very good idea what the answer to that might be.

He hesitated, then went on, a smile twinkling in his blue eyes. "Because I know that a local television station owns that condo. They usually use it for visiting celebrities or out-of-town guests or…" He let it hang.

She didn't. "Or?" she demanded, eyes flashing, challenging him. *Come on, come on. Say it.*

"Or girlfriends of the executives," he said at last, his eyes laughing at her.

Of course. That must have been what Bambi was. And how many other station floozies before her? How convenient for Jack to have that sort of woman living next door, whole streams of them, one right after another. No wonder he'd felt at home walking right into her yard the way he had. He was used to making himself at home.

"Sorry, mister," she said icily. "No such luck."

He smiled, his eyes twinkling. "Don't worry, J.J., I never for a moment doubted your virtue. It's written all over you."

"So that's why you offered me the nanny job last night," she said musingly. "I see. Just to make sure I had an honorable way to make a living."

He laughed, genuinely amused by her tone. "You do have a quaint and rather judgmental way of putting things."

She was about to make a smart-aleck remark and maybe even call him a name, but Annie came out of the kitchen just in time and she had to be on her best behavior in front of the child. Quickly she suppressed her outrage and got herself back on the track of pleasant conversation.

"Good morning, Annie," she said, smiling at her. "Are you ready to go?"

The little girl nodded solemnly and put on her coat. "I'm ready," she said, taking J.J.'s hand as though she knew how to do these things. "I'll show you where my school is."

"Good." J.J. looked back at Jack and resisted the impulse to stick out her tongue at him.

He grinned, reading her mind once again, and she left with a snap to her walk. His grin turned into soft laughter as the door closed behind her. She was a cutie.

And that reminded him. He'd promised himself he was going to put away that picture of Phoebe that stood on his dresser. The picture Annie kept would always be out, and he knew it. That was the way it had to be. But his picture would be packed away. Phoebe was dead, and he was finally ready to put the memories, good and bad, away where they belonged. Turning, he headed for his bedroom to do the deed.

The school was close by and J.J. drove Annie up to the entrance, then watched as she ran in with the other children. By now she was almost half an hour late to work and she knew she was going to have to pay one way or another. But it was worth it. Annie was a quiet and serious child, but there was something in her J.J. responded to. She didn't mind at all doing things for her.

Her father was another story. But she didn't have time to think about that now. She had to get her work face on and her mind focused—and forget all about the infuriating man next door.

She had to turn down lunch with a group of her new co-workers, but she made it back to the school just before twelve-thirty. The mothers were gathered around the bottom of the stairs, waiting for the kindergartners to come down, and J.J. slipped out of her car and joined them.

Most of these women were her age, some of them younger. This might have been her if she'd chosen another direction to her life. Looking at these women, she noted their easy camaraderie, their sense of community, but she didn't feel any regret. Their way was fine for them, but not for her. Staying at home with children every day—how could they stand it?

The little ones began to come down the stairs in a line, one behind the next. They were so short, like pint-sized people, and so cute with their bobbed hair and eager round faces.

Most of them carried big colorful paintings and called to their mothers as they came toward them, the girls skipping, the boys swaggering just a little. She caught sight of Annie and waved. The girl's face lit up for just a second, then went solemn again, as though she didn't want to give away too much of her own emotion.

Poor thing, J.J. thought. *What are you saving it for?*

Annie sat in the passenger's seat, her legs stuck straight out, and showed J.J. the picture she'd drawn with big fat crayons.

"It's an elephant," she said proudly. "See the trunk?"

It looked more like a mouse in a Halloween mask, but J.J. nodded and praised it. "Be sure to show that to your daddy," she said, smiling at the simple pride the girl had in her work.

"I will," Annie replied. "I didn't make it for him."

"Oh?" J.J. murmured abstractedly as she made the turn into the condo parking lot. "Whom did you make it for?"

"My new mother," Annie said matter-of-factly. "I save all my pictures for her. They're in a drawer in my room."

J.J. turned to look at her, surprised. "Is...is your daddy getting married again?" she said before she thought, then wished she'd kept her mouth shut. After all, it was none of her business if he was.

But Annie shook her head, her eyes dark and unreadable.

"Not yet," she said cryptically, then pushed on the door handle and slipped out of the car.

J.J. followed, a sick feeling growing in the pit of her stomach. There was no new mother, was there? Not even on the horizon. And this little girl wanted one desperately.

The sadness of her situation was scary. J.J. had never dealt with the sort of deep, lasting emotion Annie must be experiencing, and she only wished she knew of something she could do to help her.

But wait, she thought to herself. What was she thinking? Of course she'd dealt with it. She'd gone through something similar herself. Why was she blocking that out of her memories?

This child will be scarred for life, she thought to herself as she watched Annie running for her home. A hollow pain, well hidden and deeply held, twisted inside her. *Am I scarred?* she asked herself wonderingly. *Am I twisted and hurt beyond mending?*

Not so you'd notice. At least, not at first glance. So she was ambitious rather than wanting a family and all that came with it—so what? That didn't mean anything. Lots of women chose careers over children these days. Lots and lots.

Yeah, and look at their happy faces.

J.J. jumped. It was almost as though someone had made that sarcastic statement aloud. But no. It had come from her own traitorous mind. She shook herself and hurried after Annie. This mental conversation was getting ridiculous.

Annie was standing on tiptoes to turn the knob on her condo door. Her little fingers curled around it and her face was red with the effort. And then the door was open and suddenly her face lit up.

"Marguerite! You're back," she called out, and forgetting all about J.J., she disappeared into the house.

J.J. stopped dead and wavered for a moment. Ordinarily she would go to the door and make sure everything was okay. But something about that dismissal from Annie's attention span cut a bit, and she decided it wasn't necessary this time. Things seemed to be under control. The fabled Marguerite was back and she was definitely a force to be reckoned with.

"Well," she said quietly to herself, turning and heading for her own doorway. "That takes care of that. Now that the wonderful Marguerite has returned, they won't need me at all."

Which was exactly the way she wanted it to be. So why did she feel so empty inside? She turned the key in her lock and the door swung open.

She was nearly inside when she heard Jack call to her. Turning back, she watched him coming down the walk and she frowned, not sure why he was intent upon prolonging this. After all, every time they were together, they ended up in an argument. Who needed that? She would just as soon he left her alone.

But he wasn't going to do that.

As he came down the stairs, he could read the wariness on her face. She looked like a cornered lioness, wanting to flee but ready to fight if she had to. He liked that. If she didn't watch out she would begin to present a challenge to him. A challenge he couldn't resist. And that could be quite dangerous—for them both.

"Wait a minute," he said, meeting her in her doorway. "I want to thank you for your help today."

She shook her head, dismissing it and starting to back into her entryway, her gaze veiled. "No need. It was no big deal."

"Sure it was," he said easily, following her into her room, although she was giving off obvious body language that he was definitely not invited in. "The last thing I'd want to do is keep Annie home to help me. Without you, I would have had to."

She steeled herself against sympathy, and she left the door open as a major hint, turning to glare at him as he sauntered into her kitchen. He was dressed in snug-fitting jeans and a blue jersey shirt that looked as though it had shrunk in the wash. The fit was perfect for showing off his surprisingly muscular body. She wondered, fleetingly, when he found time to work out. A man who stayed home watching babies all day shouldn't look this good.

He turned and caught her gaze before she could hide it, and he saw the reluctant admiration there.

The feeling is mutual, he told her silently with a trace of a smile, and she flushed, but he didn't stop looking.

She was definitely good to look at. He'd spent most of his life in a profession where youth and beauty were idealized, and no one knew better than he how shallow young, pretty people could be. She'd probably been pretty as a twenty-one-year-old, and she still was, but there was more to her than that. There was character in her face, a kind of honesty, an awareness a younger woman didn't often have.

She had depth, J.J. did. He liked depth. Now, why exactly didn't she like him?

"I won't stay long," he told her reassuringly. In some ways, he was taking a break, escaping, and she was somewhere to go. But as his gaze skimmed over her face, he knew it was more than that. He'd watched her that morning on the television and she intrigued him. There was something about her....

"And you can go ahead and close the door without worrying," he added, holding up his hands as though to show he had no weapons. "I'm not going to attack you."

"I know that," she said defensively, but she didn't move to close the door.

He searched her gaze for a moment, finding nothing but barricades, and sighed, shaking his head.

"Relax," he told her softly. "I'll go. It's obvious you don't want me here." He started toward the open door, but she felt a quick stab of remorse and she followed, touching his arm, stopping him.

"No, wait," she said. "I . . . I'm sorry." She shrugged, glancing at his shirt, avoiding his eyes. "I'm tired and I'm in a bad mood. I guess I've been taking it out on you."

Lame excuses and she knew it, but what else could she say? She had been acting rudely, and she didn't want to be like that. Swallowing hard, she forced herself to give him a tiny smile.

"Come on in. For just a minute, anyway."

He turned back slowly, then looked down into her eyes. They were still stormy. "Are you sure?"

She nodded, and he smiled at her. She didn't really want him here, but if he left, they might never get beyond hostility. He decided to stay.

"Would you like something to drink?" she asked stiffly.

He shook his head. "No thanks."

She gestured for him to come on into her home and he started into the living room, looking about with interest. Nothing had changed. The odds and ends that had decorated the bookcases and shelves during Bambi's stay were still in place. J.J. was obviously just using the place temporarily. Turning back, he noted she was finally closing her front door.

He looked at her steadily as she came along to join him in the living room, thinking what a respite she was from his daily routine. He knew he'd come to visit her mainly because he'd had to get away. It had been a lousy day, one of those black cloud exercises in horror that came every now and then. Some days were like a miracle of joy with his children. Others were like today—just plain bad. On days like today, the guilty wish he could escape came over him like a disease.

He always fought it. So far, he'd always been successful in fighting it, and he didn't have any plans to give in to the malaise. But there were times when he needed a few minutes away from the babies, with an adult to talk to. And right now, gazing at this pretty woman, he felt like a man just off the desert taking a long, cool drink of water. This was just what he'd needed.

He had no ulterior motives. He just needed to be here.

"It's been a rough morning," he murmured, more to himself than to her.

But she heard it, and she groaned silently. He was doing it. He was going to get to her, pull her chain, make her feel things she didn't want to feel. She didn't want to sympathize with him and his plight. She didn't want to feel an urgent need to help. She wanted to stay out of his life if she could. Tossing her hair, she looked at the couch, wondering how long she could go before she would have to give in and invite him to sit down.

She looked back at him again. He was waiting. The question was in his eyes. And suddenly, she felt like laughing. This whole situation was funny, really. They were like two kids who'd been forced to go to a party where neither one of them wanted to dance.

"Well, you have Marguerite back now," she noted pertly. "Things should be better."

He raised an eyebrow. "Should they? But you haven't met Marguerite yet, have you?" He turned and studied her. Why was she acting like the cat that ate the canary? It wasn't mockery, really, but something close to it. "It is a relief to have her back, actually," he admitted.

She folded her arms across her chest and looked at him coolly. It wasn't considered hip to be morally indignant, but what the heck. She'd never worried about what was in vogue. "I imagine it is," she said with a slight—though very feminine—sneer.

He almost laughed at the haughty picture she made, but he knew instinctively that would be the kiss of death. Instead, he looked away and gestured toward the couch.

"Mind if I sit down? I've got something I want to discuss with you."

"Why?" she asked pointedly. "Surely you're not going to offer me another job. You don't need me any longer." She waved a dismissive hand in the air. "You've got Marguerite."

He stared at her, puzzled. Marguerite knew everything there was to know about babies and was a fair-to-middling cook, but J.J. was acting almost as though she were jealous of her. The thought made him grin.

"Believe me," he drawled, watching her eyes. "Marguerite can't do it all."

J.J.'s eyes widened with mock innocence. "Oh, really?"

This was getting them nowhere. He was going to have to change the subject. At the same time, it was evident she was ignoring his request to sit, so he pretended he hadn't noticed the lack of an invitation and sat anyway. She followed him, sitting gingerly on a chair across from the couch, and he smiled at her.

"Now this has been bothering me all day. I watched you on the news this morning, and the feeling is growing stronger all the time." His eyes narrowed and his head went back. "We've met before, haven't we? Where do I know you from?"

Her heart was beating just a little faster. This was exactly what she'd been afraid of. She didn't want to remind him. There was hardly anything to it, but what there was was too embarrassing. She was going to try to avoid revealing their previous meetings at all costs.

"I'm in the same business you used to be in," she said evasively, and tried to think of a quick way to change the subject. She glanced at him with his anchorman good looks and cocked an eyebrow. "And what I'd like to know is why you don't seem to be in it anymore."

His own eyes darkened. He hadn't expected her to know of his background in the business. Unless, of course, they really had met before, which he had a feeling was entirely possible.

"Who said I wasn't?" he asked softly.

She hesitated. "Well, you're not working at any of the local stations. Are you?"

She did know him from somewhere if she knew his work. It had been a good three years since he'd been on camera anywhere. That was a long time in this business. People forgot you after six weeks in some places. He nodded slowly.

"That's right."

"And from talking to other people," she continued, "I gather you haven't been on the air for a number of years."

He shrugged. "That's partly right." And he gazed at her again, trying to figure out where he might have known her.

She waited a second or two, but he didn't continue, and she added another question, "Why not?"

He met her gaze and held it. "There are a lot of reasons why not."

She swallowed, wishing he would leave, wishing this conversation were not even happening. And yet, at the same time, she really did want to know the answers to her questions. She had been wondering, and from the talk around the station, so had a lot of people.

"The question is too personal, I know," she said quickly. "And I'm not trying to dig into your private life, but..." Her enthusiasm for her business ran away with her for the moment. "Well, I heard there is an opening in the main anchor position at a network affiliate in Salt Lake and you would be so good..."

He managed barely a ghost of a smile. This was the same thing he'd been hearing for years. There was always an opening, always someone who thought he'd be perfect. He looked away, not answering her comment.

She noticed his lack of response, but she wouldn't give up. He *had* been good. He'd been the best. Everyone had assumed he would go on to fame and glory of the highest sort. So what could possibly be the problem?

"Do you think you'll ever go back?" she asked him.

Involuntarily he winced. No. He didn't. But he wasn't going to tell her that. And yet, the implication was clear in what he did say to her.

"I can't predict the future. But it isn't in my dreams."

She sat forward in her chair, still eager to urge him on in what she knew he was the best at. "Why not? You were so good, and you're still so... still so..."

"Still so what?" His irrepressible smile took over. "Still able to articulate a three-syllable word without stuttering? Still able to get through lunch without drooling on my bib?"

She'd been going to say still so good-looking, but she flushed, unable to say the words, knowing he would find them shallow and less than flattering. "I'm... I'm just curious why you don't want to jump back into the business if there's a chance."

"I have four kids to raise," he said shortly. "When do you suggest I go in to do a news show? Between the breakfast feeding and the morning nap? That is, if I can get all three of the triplets to sleep at the same time. Or maybe before they wake up in the morning. That might give me an hour or so before sunrise."

He stopped himself, knowing he was sounding a little too defensive. Shaking his head, he added more gently, "I'm afraid I'm a little too busy for that."

"Oh, I know that. But plenty of single mothers go back to work. Surely you could arrange child care. Mothers seem to work it out."

"Not if they have triplets they don't."

She bit her lip, knowing he was probably right. She'd seen the chaos three demanding babies could conjure up. But she hated to think of him never going back to broadcasting. The entire business would be poorer if he never returned.

"Don't worry, J.J.," he said softly, interested and a bit touched that she seemed to care this much. "I made enough while I was working, and invested it wisely, so I can take these years off with impunity. I'm going to be okay, and so is the television industry. Life goes on." He gazed at her levelly for a moment, then gave her a quick smile.

"Actually, the only way I would ever go back into the business would be with my own station in some small town somewhere—an operation I could control on my own, from the news in the morning to the cooking show in the afternoon to the late night movie."

"With you playing all the parts?" she asked, incredulous.

"Why not?"

"That's really turning back the clock, isn't it? That sounds like stations in the fifties."

"It's still possible in some remote markets, especially with cable."

She shook her head, marveling. This man could have been on top of the world, and instead, he wanted to be in some little out-of-the-way town, doing…well, doing what he liked to do. That thought gave her pause. Maybe he wasn't so crazy after all.

"Isn't Bob Newton still the station manager?" he asked her. "How is old Bob? I used to work with him in San Francisco."

They chatted about the personnel at the station for a few moments. He knew a few of the upper management, though the younger workers were all new to him. Still, he'd never made the effort to contact anyone. It had been pure coincidence that he'd bought a condo right next to the one the station owned, and the people he'd met who'd stayed there had generally kept his presence confidential. He wasn't sure why. He'd never asked anyone to do that. They all seemed to have sensed the fact that he didn't much want to advertise his whereabouts and they respected his privacy.

But maybe that was a mistake. Maybe he'd had too much privacy of late. He didn't know if that was true, but he did know something was wrong. He was happy. He adored his children and he was bound and determined to do his best by them. But there was something else.

He stirred, shifting his position. He was going through a restless period, that was all. At least, he hoped that was all.

He looked at J.J. She was talking about plans for a new magazine show at the station, but he wasn't really listening to her. His gaze was lingering on the way her lips moved when she said the words, the way her creamy skin contrasted with the velvet black of her hair, the way her thick lashes shadowed her dark eyes, and he felt the hot, liquid surge of need begin to grow deep inside. He wanted her. He wanted this woman in a way he hadn't felt for years, not for any woman since...

Grimacing, he shifted his position and forced his gaze out toward the mountains. This was no way for a father of four little ones to act, for God's sake. He was going to have to keep better control than this.

J.J. went on talking, and now just the sound of her voice was raising the hair on the back of his neck. This was crazy. Abruptly he stood and walked to the sliding glass door. He opened it and walked onto the patio deck, breathing deeply into the cool air, staring up at the red cliffs.

J.J. watched him, her mouth pursed cynically. *Go ahead and make yourself at home,* she thought as she rose to join him, but aloud she said, "I'm sure this place must look familiar to you. From what you told me, you've been a regular visitor."

He turned to look at her, his eyes hooded in a strange way that startled her. "Did I say that?" he asked.

She blinked. Something in his look, in his voice, was setting off alarms all through her system.

"Well, you did . . . and your daughter."

"Oh." He turned back toward the mountains. "She was talking about Bambi."

Who else? J.J. grimaced and shrugged. "As I remember, that was the name she mentioned."

He nodded absently. "Yes, Bambi was a good friend."

"I see."

"No, I don't think you do."

He'd heard the veiled sarcasm in her voice and he looked at her with a sparkle in his blue eyes. This wasn't the first time she'd hinted at things she didn't seem to want to come right out and say.

"Has anyone ever told you that you have a dirty mind?" he asked her.

Her head jerked up and she stared into his eyes. "What?"

He moved closer, looking down at her with an intensity she wasn't used to. "You think every relationship I have with a woman has got to somehow involve erotic activities. Don't you?"

She was turning red again. Would that be so surprising? Ten years ago he'd had a reputation as a playboy. Why would he have changed? "I never said that," she claimed, avoiding his gaze.

"No, not in so many words, but you didn't have to. The tone of your voice said it, the look in your face, the set of your shoulders, they said it all."

She was thoroughly embarrassed now. He certainly had a knack. She turned to leave him there, but he caught hold of her elbow with his large hand, holding her in place before him.

"You know, there's a theory that we most often suspect others of doing things we're likely to do ourselves," he told her softly, his hard gaze studying her face. "Or want to do, but don't dare."

She looked up into his deep, dark blue eyes and wanted to run. "You're making that up," she said weakly.

His fingers tightened. "Why? Do you deny it?"

Her heart was pounding and she prayed he couldn't tell. But how could he avoid it? To her, it sounded like a drum being beaten in her ear.

"Me?" she protested. "What do I have to deny?"

He pulled her closer, forcing her to look up into his face. "You have this idea in your head that I'm some sort of wicked degenerate. I don't know where you got it. And I don't know what I can possibly do to prove to you that I'm not what you think. Do you have any suggestions?"

He was too close and a sudden wave of shivering excitement swept over her. Unable to speak, she shook her head and tried to think of a way to get him to stop touching her. Somehow, just jerking her arm away from his grip didn't enter her mind. So she stood very still and hardly breathed.

"I'll be honest with you, J.J.," he continued when she didn't answer. His voice was low and husky, and the sound from it seemed to vibrate against her skin.

"It's been a long, long time since I've kissed a woman, and looking down into your beautiful face, with that soft, pink mouth and the way wisps of hair are falling over your eyes, the urge to take you in my arms and find out if I can still remember how to make love to a woman is so strong, it stings."

She was paralyzed, frozen where she stood, and his free hand came up and brushed one of the wisps away from her cheek, touching her so gently, it felt like a feather.

"You are the most tempting thing to come into my range in a long time," he murmured at last, looking regretfully at her mouth. "It might be better if you stayed away from me."

Then a bitter smile twisted his handsome face and he dropped her elbow, turning on his heel and striding for the door. She stayed where she was, listening as the door closed behind him, and then, finally she felt as though she could breathe again.

"Wow," she whispered to herself. "If only..."

If only, what? She wasn't sure what came next in that sentence, and she wasn't even sure she wanted to know.

Five

For the next few days, J.J. avoided Jack like the plague, ducking into her apartment quickly on her way home, staying away from public areas when she knew there might be a chance that he would show up. But for some reason, she couldn't avoid his spirit. When she was in the condo, he was only a few hundred yards away. There were walls between them, but that hardly seemed to matter. Lying awake at night, she could feel him in the next room, sense his presence as though it were a sound, a scent, a movement that affected her airspace.

The sense of him even affected her at work when she was on camera, giving the news. She was sure, somehow, that he was at home, watching her, and that made her feel stiff and awkward. No one mentioned it; in fact, everyone praised her work. They didn't seem to notice that she was self-conscious in a way she'd never been before on the air.

To make matters worse, she couldn't stop thinking about Annie. She kept picturing the little girl next door doing all that work, like a miniature woman, taking care of a man and three babies when she was hardly more than a baby herself, and with no help from anyone but the remarkable Marguerite. Her sad eyes haunted J.J. If only there was something she could do for the girl without getting involved with Jack.

She had to get her head on straight again. She'd come here to advance her career. Her focus should be on that one hundred percent of the time. Though, actually, things seemed to be chugging along fairly smoothly in that department. Everyone said they liked her work. She'd been handed a plum investigative story, uncovering a plot by some people living in a boardinghouse nearby to claim dogs as dependents on their tax forms. She'd gone live on the scene amid lots of barking and braying and leaping Yorkshires, and her questioning had caused one of the women to confess on the air. The ratings had been great. But had the network been watching? Who knew.

During her stay at the condo, she inadvertently found some clues as to how Jack kept himself in such great shape. He swam laps, early in the morning before most people were up.

Though the weather was still chilly, people did use the community pool in the center of the condo courtyard. The pool was heated and steam rose from it on cool mornings, reminding her of scenes from Dante's Inferno. She left for the station at daybreak, and just as she was getting into her car, a figure loomed through the mist. It was Jack, and he'd just pulled himself up out of the pool. With water still dripping, he reached for a towel, but before he covered up she saw more of that magnificent body, and she sat paralyzed for two or three minutes, before she could gather her wits together enough to start the engine and get going toward work.

She died a thousand deaths hoping he hadn't noticed her sitting there, staring at him. But the reaction had been beyond her control, and even now, as the picture of that body swam into her memory's eye, she gasped and shook her head. Those wide, muscular shoulders, those tight, narrow hips, those sculpted legs—she groaned. A man didn't have a right to be that gorgeous. It just wasn't fair.

She tried dating Martin, the sportscaster, but that was a washout. He talked about nothing but baseball statistics, and she just wasn't in the mood. He kissed her passionately at her door and all she could think about was how to find out what kind of toothpaste he used, because he tasted so minty fresh. She ignored his hints about being asked in and when he invited her to go to a ball game with him the next night, she turned him down, claiming too much paperwork to do at home.

Some of the other women at the station asked her out for drinks after the evening telecast, but she declined that, as well. And so she ended up wandering about the condo, trying not to listen to sounds from next door and trying to think of something to do that would take her mind off her neighbors.

She tried cleaning out the refrigerator, but she'd lived there such a short time, there wasn't much work in that. So she straightened up a stack of papers, throwing away half of them and filing the others, and while she was doing that, the invitation from Sara fell out onto the floor.

She bent down to pick it up and smiled again at the cute little duck with a ribbon around his neck. The shower was only a little over a week away now. She wished she could go.

Flipping the card open, she read the inside and immediately felt a bad case of the blues coming on. There was a certain reproach in that invitation. It was saying things to her, things like why aren't you married yet, why aren't you having a baby? She put it up on the bulletin board and stuck a pin in it with savage punctuation.

"I don't even need to call my mother," she muttered as she walked away. "My old roommates will take over the chant. Get married! Have babies! Be happy! Right."

She wasn't going to do any of those things. Not her. She had a career, didn't they all see that? She was perfectly happy. She didn't need anything else.

It was amazing how everyone wanted you to live life just the way they did. They couldn't leave room for people to follow their own stars. If they didn't do it just so, there must be something wrong with them. Well, she, for one, would go her own way.

And then there was Jack, sitting next door with all those children and no career she could see any signs of. He wasn't doing it the accepted way, either, was he? What had happened there? And why didn't he just hire someone to take care of the kids so he could get back to work? Or take them to his mother's? Those were things most men would do.

"So now who's expecting conformity," she chided herself. If she wanted to be left alone, maybe she'd better leave Jack alone, too.

If only she could.

Later that night, she lay very still with her eyes wide open, staring at the dark ceiling, listening to the sounds from the next apartment. She could hear one of the babies crying. And then she heard something else—something that sounded like a man singing. And beyond all reason, a smile came over her face, and she laughed softly before she slipped into sleep.

* * *

Jack's eyes opened and he stared into the darkness. Had he heard a baby cry? There didn't seem to be one crying now. Something else must have jerked him awake.

He glanced over at the clock at the side of his bed. Three-fifteen. A little early to get up and do his laps. But something told him he wasn't going to be falling back to sleep anytime soon. Rolling over onto his back, he put his hands behind his head and stared up at the ceiling.

"Count sheep," he told himself. "Or think about new games to play with the triplets. Or what color to paint the bathroom."

But it wasn't paint samples that came tumbling into his mind, nor was it happy hippos or little fuzzy lambs. What came to fill his mind and his senses was J.J., just as he'd known she would, just as she did every time he lay awake like this.

"Damn the woman," he muttered to himself, half chuckling. "She just won't leave me alone."

But it was his own mind that was conjuring up pictures of J.J. And that was wrong. He couldn't do that. Dallying with neighbor women was a dangerous thing to do and his instincts told him J.J. could be even more hazardous than the average seductive female of his acquaintance. A woman like that could turn a man's head around, make him forget what he was there for. And he wasn't going to do anything that might jeopardize his hold on his children. It was a pact he'd made with Annie and the babies. Maybe they wouldn't get a mother out of it, but they sure as hell would have a father, a father who never ever let them down.

So he could dream if he wanted to. But that was as far as he could let it go. And when the dreams became too intense, he had this little ritual that was becoming a tradition with him, silly as that might sound. And part of the drill was to lecture himself, and at the same time try to avoid remembering the scent of her hair.

"Get her out of your mind," he told himself sternly. "It's all animal magnetism and doesn't mean a thing unless you let it. You hardly know the woman. There's no reason to obsess about her. She'll be leaving soon, and then you'll never see her again. You're a mature man with four little kids to raise. You're committed, and there is no room in your life for pointless affairs that will only end up hurting everyone involved. So cut it out."

As usual, the lecture didn't work. He couldn't seem to shame himself enough. He needed something else.

"If only someone made a potent brand of lust-be-gone," he muttered, giving up and rising to take a cold shower. "I'd buy out the store."

But her image stayed with him right into the day, and he was so grouchy, Annie started to cry when he rebuked her for spilling her milk.

A wave of remorse swept over him immediately. "I'm so sorry, honey," he said, pulling her into his arms. "I'm being mean today, and I'm going to stop it, right now. I promise."

You see, he told himself angrily. *This is what comes from letting your libido take over your life. If lusting after the woman next door means Annie is going to be hurt, you're not going to do it.* And for a little while, that seemed to work.

He spent the morning concentrating on his kids, playing alphabet games with the triplets, helping Annie make brownies, and helping Marguerite sort the dirty wash. She walked over to the laundry room with it, leaving him alone with the children, and he pulled Kathy into his lap and rocked her while he sang softly to the three of them until Annie came running into the room.

"Daddy, Daddy, the mail is here," she cried.

He shifted the baby, who was almost asleep, to his other shoulder and craned his neck to see what Annie was holding in her little chubby hand.

"Okay, honey. What have we got?"

"A letter. Look." She dropped the ads and bills onto the floor, already able to recognize what was and what was not important.

Jack grinned. "Can you read whom it's from?" he asked her.

She squinted at the name on the return address. "I don't think so."

"Sure you can. Come on. Give it a try. What's the first letter?"

He helped her painfully sound it out syllable by syllable, until a light broke in her face and she laughed with delight. "It's from Grandpa and Grandma. Read it, Daddy. What do they say?"

"Good work, Annie." He nodded encouragement her way. "In a few months, you'll be able to read whole letters to me."

"I know," she said wisely.

He laughed, but sobered as he began to rip open the envelope. He knew what this was about. It was always the same thing. They didn't think he should stay here with the babies. They wanted him to bring the babies to live with them.

"Those children deserve more care than you can possibly give them alone" was a favorite refrain. He'd heard it before. Another one was "You're a young man and you need to get on with your life. Let the children stay with us. We have the time and the space. We can handle them."

They wanted him to come and visit, at least, and he knew they expected to be able to talk him into leaving the children once he got there. That was why he'd been avoiding the trip for so long. But he couldn't avoid it for much longer. In a little over a week, he planned to take all of them to Denver, including Marguerite. And once there, he knew he was going to have a fight on his hands.

No one was going to take his children from him. That was something that could never be, and he would fight it fiercely, with every breath in his body. He was in this for the long haul, and nobody was going to stop him—not even some sexy little cutie who filled his mind with a longing he couldn't control. No, not even her.

But just making resolutions didn't make them come true. He did pretty well through the noon feeding and for a couple of hours after that, but by late afternoon, he found himself grouchy again. His throat was scratchy and his eyes were burning and that didn't help. This time he was short with Marguerite over a missing glass, causing the babies to look up at him in surprise, their little mouths hanging open and he cursed himself and offered to go get the clean wash from the laundry room to make it up to his housekeeper.

The basket was huge—three babies used a lot of diapers in any given two-day period—and he was glad he'd gone to get it for her. But on his way back he had to pass J.J.'s door, and just as he got even with it, it shot open, surprising him, and the clean wash went flying all over the walkway and into the grass.

Diapers were falling like snowflakes. J.J. cried out and dashed about, trying to help him catch things before they reached the ground, but it was too late.

"Oh, I'm so sorry," she said over and over as she helped him pick things up. "Look, you can just brush off this grass and it's good as new." She grimaced as a grass stain refused to comply with that scenario, no matter how hard she brushed.

"Almost," she amended. "Oh, I'm so sorry. Can the babies wear something that looks like this? Oh!"

He didn't say much back. He was trying not to look at her. She was dressed for work in a tight little number that emphasized her small waist, and that in turn only emphasized how nice and round her breasts were, and how her hips would just fit in his hands like . . .

No, he wasn't going to do that.

The clothes were finally all back in the basket and they both rose and faced each other. The memory of the other night, how the heat had burned between them, was as clear as though it were being projected on a movie screen. They couldn't ignore it, and yet both were trying to do just that, trying so hard, it was visible on their faces.

"I really am sorry," she said awkwardly. "I hope . . ."

Her voice faded away and he never did get to find out what she hoped, partly because he started coughing and before he knew it, she was pounding on his back and asking him if he was choking on something.

"No," he croaked, trying to get away from her. "No, I'm okay. Stop beating me. It's just a raw throat."

"You can't afford to get sick," she said without thinking, looking concerned. "You're not sleeping enough at night. If you don't get enough sleep—"

"How did you know I wasn't sleeping?" he said before he thought, and then they were staring at each other again, realizing they were both going through the same thing.

He started to back away first, shaking his head as though he couldn't quite believe what they had just done.

"Oh no," he muttered, turning away, grabbing his basket and heading for his own front door. "Oh no, I'm not giving in to this attraction thing that easily."

He was mumbling the words to himself, but she heard enough to get the general drift, and she looked around for something to throw at him. Giving in, indeed! Who the heck did he think he was, anyway?

She found a nice big pinecone and hefted it up in her hand, but it was too late. He'd already disappeared into his condo. And all she got for her troubles was sap on her fingers.

Shaken by the entire encounter, she drove off to work, saying bad things about him under her breath. And when she read the news that night, she did it with a defiant air and a challenge in her dark eyes, meant strictly for him. Everyone said she'd never been better. But all she cared about was—had he seen it?

There was no way of knowing. She listened hard that night, but there were no sounds coming from next door. And when she finally went to sleep, she slept like a top.

She tried to call her old roommate Sara the next afternoon, to discuss the baby shower, but the number she had for her seemed to be disconnected. The shower was scheduled for a day when she was supposed to anchor the evening news. How could she ask the producer to postpone something like that? She was darn lucky they were giving her a shot at it. You couldn't say, "Oh, thanks for the invitation to dinner with the president, but I've got something else to do that day. Can we make it a week later?"

No, she wasn't going to be able to attend the shower. She tried calling another of the roommates, Cami Bishop, in Los Angeles, but found she was out of town. Driving to New Mexico, they said. That seemed like an odd thing to do, but that was Cami for you. She tried the fourth member of their group, Hailey Kingston, and got nothing there, either. Where was everyone? Suddenly she felt very much alone.

And when you feel that way, who do you call? She reached for the telephone and punched in her mother's number.

"Hi, Mom," she said hopefully when her mother answered.

"Oh, hello, dear. Is anything wrong?"

J.J.'s heart sank, recognizing the tone. Her mother was busy and didn't particularly feel like talking. Why did she keep expecting anything else?

"No. Nothing's wrong." She closed her eyes and grimaced. When would she learn not to count on anything from this quarter? "I just thought I'd call and see what you were up to."

"Well, listen, I'm glad you did call." Her mother's voice perked up. "Because your brother Jamie has a problem. He totaled his car over the weekend and of course he didn't have good insurance, so now he is really desperate. I mean, I've been driving him to work, but I have to be at the other end of town by nine and he needs a down payment before he can get another car. So I thought, since you have such a good job and you don't have any family that depends on you, you might be able to see your way clear to send him..."

Money. It always came down to that. Weren't families supposed to be there with love and understanding and emotional support? But with hers, it was always money.

She listened to the tale of woe and agreed to send her brother a check. Why not? After all, it was only money. And then she hung up and sat staring at the mountains. People wondered why she didn't have a husband, hadn't started a family of her own, and sometimes she had twinges of regret herself. But not after she'd talked to her mother. That always seemed to cure the urge.

She was moving things around in her living room for lack of anything better to do, shifting the couch to the far wall,

turning the coffee table at an angle, transferring the hall table close to the doorway—when she found a letter that must
have fallen behind the table when the previous tenant had
stacked outgoing mail there.

It was sealed, but there was no stamp. On the front, it
read "Jack Darling."

That was all. Just "Jack Darling." And yet it made her
heart sink and put a frown on her face like nothing else had
that day.

Obviously it was from that Bambi person. Probably a
love letter. Or a tome full of regrets and recriminations.
Something that would confirm his relationship with the
woman, prove emotional attachment. After all, why else
would you call a neighbor "darling"?

She was itching to read it, but she had scruples. What
good they'd ever done her she wasn't sure, but she still had
them. And she put it down on the entryway table and stared
at it—but only after holding it up to the light and making
sure you couldn't read anything through the envelope.

It was sealed tightly. There was no way to jimmy it open
and reseal it. Steaming was just a little too calculated. Besides, sometimes it left lumpy areas. So she laid it down and
she stared at it.

"I guess I'd better give it to him tomorrow," she told
herself moodily. "It might have information he should have
had by now." Who knew? She might be trying to get him to
agree to a rendezvous. Maybe the date she'd offered had already passed by. Maybe she'd waited in vain for him to
show, sitting alone in the rain.

"Too bad," J.J. said lightly, suddenly cheered. "Just too
darn bad. Better make sure your letters get delivered next
time."

She went in early to work that evening, simply to be with
people and keep from thinking. Martin told her jokes to

make her laugh and she appreciated it. Even the station manager was friendly. But she still had to go home to that empty condo with Bambi's letter to Jack sitting on the entryway table and lie in the dark, listening to the neighbors.

Six

J.J. woke up with a start. It was very late, and the babies were crying like crazy. She sat straight up in bed and listened. This was not the normal wailing for attention. There was something wrong.

Her first impulse was to run over and help. She threw off her pajamas and pulled on jeans and a sweatshirt, her nerves tingling with adrenaline, then she sat by the wall and listened again. They were still crying, but now she wasn't so sure it was anything unusual. Maybe she was imagining things. She sat very still and listened and tried to make up her mind. One thing she was pretty sure of—there was no sound of a male singing voice.

It was one o'clock in the morning, hardly the hour for a neighborly visit. And yet she couldn't go back to bed when she had this feeling that something was wrong next door. What was she afraid of—that she was going to wake them up? Who could sleep through this racket?

That tipped the balance and she was up and out of her room, heading for the front door. The nighttime air was cool and crisp and clear. It felt odd to be out when everyone else was so obviously sleeping.

Everyone but Jack's babies. The crying was even louder out on the walk and when she knocked on the door, it seemed to take those inside a long time to hear her above the noise.

Annie opened the door, her blond curls in a wild tangle, her eyes tired and her face worried.

"Annie, what on earth is going on?" J.J. cried.

She could see past the little girl into the living room. Kristi was howling at the top of her lungs, her round face red as a fire engine, her cheeks wet with tears. Baby Mack had pulled himself up into walking position, holding on to the edge of the coffee table, and was shrieking and pounding his little hands on the wood. The scene was chaotic and for poor Annie, it must have seemed hopeless.

J.J. looked down at the little girl and asked, "Where's your father? Where's Marguerite?"

But Annie seemed to be too tired to answer right away, and J.J. slipped past her, going into the room and swinging Kristi up into her arms, cooing to her as though she were an old hand at this. Still holding Kristi, she sank to sit on the coffee table and pat Baby Mack's little head.

It wasn't until later, thinking back, that she realized she did all this with no hesitation whatsoever. There was none of the reluctance to touch babies she'd felt the other day. It was as though that one inoculation had trained her enough to steam ahead with a sense of child care that almost seemed to come naturally once it had been aroused.

"Annie, what happened? Why didn't you come get help?"

"Daddy said not to," she said, sitting on the floor as though all her energy had evaporated. "Daddy's sick. He's very tired."

"Sick!" She remembered the coughing incident and glanced toward where she knew the bedrooms must be, bouncing Kristi on her lap. The baby was still crying, but now she kept putting her fist in her mouth and the sound had gone down considerably. The thought of Jack too sick to take care of the children was horrifying. Who else could handle them?

"Annie, what is the matter with him?" she asked worriedly.

"I don't know." Her huge eyes were tragic. "Marguerite got sick, too. Her sister came and took her away."

"What?" J.J.'s sense of horror was growing. "And you've been here all alone with your sick father and these babies? Oh, Annie." She gave the child a pitying look, but there was no time to waste in sympathy. She swung Kristi back up against her shoulder and rose.

"Where is your father?" she asked.

"In there." Annie pointed at a doorway, and J.J. went toward it quickly.

There was Jack, fully dressed and seemingly out cold on the bed, with Kathy crawling over him and whimpering. J.J.'s heart fell and she dashed over and put a hand to his forehead. He was burning up.

His eyes shot open. "Oh. Hi," he said, and began to try to struggle upright.

"You stay where you are," she told him firmly. "Why didn't you call me? Why didn't you tell me things were this bad?"

"Bad?" He blinked at her, looking bleary and puzzled. "Nothing's that bad. I just had to take a little rest, that's all. I'll be okay in a minute."

He sank back against the pillows and she stood over him, shaking her head.

"You're sick as a dog," she told him, exasperated and sympathetic, all at the same time. "And you shouldn't be anywhere near these babies."

"I'll be okay," he insisted weakly, squinting as though he were having a hard time seeing her clearly. "I shouldn't have taken that medicine. Just let me rest a minute, and I'll..."

He couldn't even finish the sentence. She stared down at him in dismay. The babies were crying, Marguerite was gone, and Jack was down like a tree in a storm.

Realization hit her. As the only functioning adult left standing, she was going to have to take over. What choice did she have? She was going to have to make a few decisions. And those decisions were going to have to come on the fly, because she didn't have a clue as to what you did with a bunch of sick people. In her book, you called a doctor and let an expert take over. But this was the middle of the night, and she supposed Jack wasn't actually near death. And if none of the babies had yet begun to come down with whatever this was, the doctor could wait until morning.

"Okay," she muttered. "First decision. We'll call the doctor in the morning."

The next thing was to get the babies down and back to sleep. Still holding Kristi in her left arm, she pulled Kathy up in her right and carried them both away from their very sick father. Surprisingly, they both quieted, craning their little round heads back to stare at her, but they seemed to recognize her and accept her.

Annie had Baby Mack, but the poor girl was so tired, she could hardly carry him. J.J. made another decision. The babies were going down in their beds, and if they were going to cry, that was just too bad. Annie needed to get some sleep, or soon she would be out with this illness, as well. It just wasn't fair to expect her to stay up caring for babies.

All three were in their pajamas, though Kathy had a dirty diaper and needed to be changed. J.J. kept Annie up long enough to show her about changing, then popped Kathy, along with her sister and brother, into their cribs, kissed each one on the top of the head, turned on the night-light, and left the room, closing the door behind her.

There was stunned silence for a moment, as though they couldn't believe she would actually be doing such a thing as this, and then the angry howls began. J.J. wanted to cover her ears. Each voice was a knife in her heart. But what could she do? It was three against one, and she couldn't fight those odds right now.

She found Annie falling asleep on the couch, her blond curls falling over her eyes. She smiled at the picture the little darling made and picked her up, carrying her into the third bedroom, which she assumed, by the pictures of Disney characters on the wall, must be hers. The child was groggy with exhaustion and she helped her change into her nightgown, then tucked her into bed.

"The babies are still crying," Annie murmured, her eyes closing involuntarily.

"Don't you pay any attention to that," J.J. told her, stroking her cheek and smiling down at her. "You get some sleep. Tomorrow's Saturday, so you have no school and I don't have to go to work. You just sleep as late as you want. I'll take care of things."

"Okay," she whispered, and in less time than it took to say it, she was asleep, her golden lashes long and curved against chubby pink cheeks.

J.J. turned off her light and left her door ajar. As she came out into the living room, she realized a miracle had happened. The babies had stopped crying. They might even be asleep.

"Worn out by all this commotion, no doubt," she muttered to herself. And they weren't the only ones.

She looked around the room and wondered what she was going to do next. Jack was still in a semi-coma on his bed. What he really needed to do was get out of here, like Marguerite had. He was undoubtedly contagious, and the fact that he probably had been for days already didn't make any difference. He should still get away from them, just in case. And how was she going to manage to get that taken care of?

This was really strange. In a matter of minutes, she'd gone from being a carefree single woman with no one depending on her to finding herself in charge of a house full of babies and a sick man. If anyone had warned her this was about to happen, she would have run in another direction. But now that she'd been thrust into the middle of it, she had to admit, she was rather excited by the challenge.

Still, was she up to it? And what was she going to do about Jack?

J.J. was still puzzling that out when a soft rap sounded on the front door. She went to it immediately and found a middle-aged, kindly looking woman standing outside, dressed in silks and long strands of gold jewelry and looking as though she'd just come from a formal event.

"Hello, dear," she said to J.J., pushing back her thick, graying black hair. "I'm Mrs. Lark. I live across the way."

J.J. nodded. She recognized the woman. They often passed in the parking lot.

But Mrs. Lark had not yet made the connection. "Did Jack hire you from the agency?" she asked. "He said he was going to call and try to get someone. I just got back from a Las Vegas trip and I promised I would look in on the babies, and since your light was still on, I thought I'd take a chance. How are they?''

"The babies are all right, but Jack isn't very well. He's pretty sick, in fact.'' She gave the woman a fleeting smile. "I'm J. J. Jensen, from next door.''

Mrs. Lark's eyebrows rose as she recognized her. "Of course you are. I've seen you often.''

"You knew Jack and Marguerite were sick?'' J.J. asked, ushering the woman into the entryway.

"Oh, yes. I usually stop by to see how things are going about once a day. It's such a job that man has taken on, you know. I feel as though his friends must support him.'' She shook her head, thinking about his situation. Her eyes held affection and concern for her neighbor, and J.J. was struck by that. Obviously this woman didn't think Jack was a scoundrel at all.

"And I did talk to him earlier today,'' Mrs. Lark continued. "They had a bad night last night, I know. Have things gotten worse?''

J.J. nodded, pulling her arms in close. At first, she'd felt a sense of relief when Mrs. Lark knocked. Finally there was someone else to help shoulder this load. But as she talked to her, she began to realize she didn't really want to share it with someone else. For some reason, she felt as though it were her place to help Jack and Annie. Mrs. Lark was very nice, but she wasn't as intimately attached to the family.

And you are? her inner voice scoffed. But she didn't want to listen to it.

"Actually, things have gotten worse,'' she told Mrs. Lark. "Marguerite was so ill, her sister came to take her home. And Jack—well, he's in the bedroom.'' She had a thought and looked at the lady speculatively. "I know it's awfully late, but perhaps you could help me here.''

"Of course, dear," the woman said kindly. "I was planning to come spend the night if they needed me, and it seems they do."

J.J. appreciated the woman's eagerness to help, but she hesitated. She was planning to stay, herself. She didn't really think they needed two women sitting up all night waiting for something to happen.

"You know, I don't think that will be necessary. But I would like to get Jack away from the babies. I was thinking that if you could stay with the babies for a little bit, I could get him over to my condo next door."

"Your condo?" There was a look of surprise on the kindly woman's face that made J.J. scramble with her explanation.

"Yes, only not to stay with me," she said quickly. "I'll leave him there where he can have some peace and quiet, and I'll come back over here to stay with the children. And then you can go home."

Mrs. Lark looked a little skeptical. "Well, of course, dear. If you think so. I'm glad to help in any way I can."

J.J. smiled at her. "Great. I'll just see if I can get Jack up and out of here."

The older woman hovered after her. "Do you think you'll need me to help you with him?" she asked.

J.J. looked from Mrs. Lark in to the bedroom and back again. She had no idea how she was going to do this.

"I don't think so," she said, though she hadn't a clue. "I'll let you know. If you just sit down and listen for the babies, that will be help enough."

Mrs. Lark nodded and sat on the couch, picking up a magazine.

J.J. started for the bedroom, her pulse beating faster with every step she took. Sick or not, Jack was not going to go easily. She knew that for sure. He had a fierce attachment to his children that she hadn't really understood before, but now that she thought back, she knew it was true. What if he wouldn't go?

She entered the darkened bedroom carefully. He seemed to be sound asleep. She stood over him for a moment, just taking in the scene. Dressed in a sweater and dark slacks, he was lying atop the covers, on his back, with one arm thrown over his eyes. Even sick, he looked awfully good.

"Jack," she said softly, shaking his shoulder. "Jack."

He moved his arm and gazed up at her with a confused frown. "J.J.," he said, his voice slurred. "I'm dreaming, right?"

"No, Jack. You're not dreaming." She sank down to sit beside him on the bed.

He turned and blinked at her, up on one elbow. "Then I must be delirious," he muttered, and suddenly his hand shot out and his fingers curled around her wrist. "Hmm. Feels real."

She hesitated, looking down at his hand on her arm, but she didn't push him away. After all, he was a sick man. What could she do?

"Jack, I'm real. Now listen to me. You're very sick. I think you ought to go stay in my condo until you're better."

A ghost of a smile settled on his wide mouth. "Ah, then I *am* dreaming," he said softly, and his eyelids drooped as though he could barely stay awake. "If I close my eyes, do you promise not to disappear?"

"Try to stay awake, Jack." She shook his shoulder gently, and his eyes opened again. "We have to talk. You're too sick to take care of these children and anyway, you're probably contagious."

Dear Reader,

YOU MAY BE A MAILBOX AWAY FROM BEING OUR NEW MILLION $$ WINNER!

Scratch off the gold on Game Cards 1-7 to automatically qualify for a chance to win a cash prize of up to $1 Million in lifetime cash! Do the same on Game Cards 8 & 9 to automatically get free books and a free surprise gift -- and to try Silhouette's no-risk Reader Service. It's a delightful way to get our best novels each month -- at discount -- with no obligation to buy, ever. Here's how it works, satisfaction fully guaranteed:

After receiving your free books, if you don't want any more, just write "cancel" on the accompanying statement, and return it to us. If you do not cancel, each month we'll send you 6 additional novels to read and enjoy & bill you just $3.24 each plus 25¢ delivery and applicable sales tax, if any.* That's the complete price, and -- compared to cover prices of $3.99 each -- quite a bargain!

You may cancel at any time, but if you choose to continue, every month we'll send you 6 more books, which you may either purchase at the discount price...or return to us and cancel your subscription.

P.S. Don't Forget to include your Bonus Token.

SEE BACK OF BOOK FOR SWEEPSTAKES DETAILS. ENTER TODAY, AND... *Good Luck!*

▲ CAREFULLY PRE-FOLD & TEAR ALONG DOTTED LINES, MOISTEN & FOLD OVER FLAP TO SEAL REPLY ▲

Win $ TRIPLE LUCK Lotto

Up To $1,000,000

GAME CARD **2**

Scratch off Gold Panel on tickets 1-7 until at least 5 (hearts) are revealed on one ticket. Doing so makes you eligible for a chance to win one of the following prizes: Grand Prize, $1,000,000.00; 1st Prize, $50,000.00; 2nd Prize, $10,000.00; 3rd Prize, $5,000.00; 4th Prize, $1,000.00; 5th Prize, $250.00; 6th Prize, $10.00.

Win $ TRIPLE LUCK Lotto

Up To $1,000,000

GAME CARD **5**

Scratch off Gold Panel on tickets 1-7 until at least 5 (hearts) are revealed on one ticket. Doing so makes you eligible for a chance to win one of the following prizes: Grand Prize, $1,000,000.00; 1st Prize, $50,000.00; 2nd Prize, $10,000.00; 3rd Prize, $5,000.00; 4th Prize, $1,000.00; 5th Prize, $250.00; 6th Prize, $10.00.

Win $ TRIPLE LUCK Lotto

For FREE BOOKS

GAME CARD **8**

Scratch off the Gold Panel. You will receive one FREE BOOK for each ★ that appears. See the back of this Game Card for details.

Win$ TRIPLE LUCKY Lotto

Up To $1,000,000

Scratch off Gold Panel on tickets 1-7 until at least 5 (hearts) are revealed on one ticket. Doing so makes you eligible for a chance to win one of the following prizes: Grand Prize, $1,000,000.00; 1st Prize, $50,000.00; 2nd Prize, $10,000.00; 3rd Prize, $5,000.00; 4th Prize, $1,000.00; 5th Prize, $250.00; 6th Prize, $10.00.

ALL PRIZES GUARANTEED TO BE AWARDED

GAME CARD 1

Win$ TRIPLE LUCKY Lotto

Up To $1,000,000

Scratch off Gold Panel on tickets 1-7 until at least 5 (hearts) are revealed on one ticket. Doing so makes you eligible for a chance to win one of the following prizes: Grand Prize, $1,000,000.00; 1st Prize, $50,000.00; 2nd Prize, $10,000.00; 3rd Prize, $5,000.00; 4th Prize, $1,000.00; 5th Prize, $250.00; 6th Prize, $10.00.

ALL PRIZES GUARANTEED TO BE AWARDED

GAME CARD 4

Win$ TRIPLE LUCKY Lotto

Up To $1,000,000

Scratch off Gold Panel on tickets 1-7 until at least 5 (hearts) are revealed on one ticket. Doing so makes you eligible for a chance to win one of the following prizes: Grand Prize, $1,000,000.00; 1st Prize, $50,000.00; 2nd Prize, $10,000.00; 3rd Prize, $5,000.00; 4th Prize, $1,000.00; 5th Prize, $250.00; 6th Prize, $10.00.

ALL PRIZES GUARANTEED TO BE AWARDED

GAME CARD 7

DETACH & RETURN ALL 9 CARDS INTACT. FOLD TWICE & MAIL WITH EXTRA BONUS TOKEN IN POSTAGE PAID ENVELOPE ▼

"The kids." Dropping her wrist, he started to force himself to sit up. "I've got to go see about the kids."

"Never mind." She gently shoved him back down, amazed at how easily she could push him around. He really had to be sick to let her get away with this.

"The children are all asleep. They're fine. Mrs. Lark is out in the living room. She'll sit with them while I take you to my place."

This business about going to her condo seemed to be very puzzling for him. He frowned, trying hard to get it straight, but it was just too unbelievable to grasp.

"I'm going back to sleep," he muttered, rolling over and closing his eyes. "Good night."

She sighed, leaning over him. "I wish I could let you do that, but I can't. This is the perfect time to make the exchange, since we have Mrs. Lark here."

She touched him again, pushing back his tousled hair and smoothing it away from his forehead. Funny how she would never have done such a thing if he were well. But with him sick and groggy, she felt free to indulge her impulses.

"I'm afraid I'm going to have to get you up on your feet and moving. Come on." She shook his shoulder again. "Let's go."

He opened his eyes and turned to look at her. She grabbed his hand and began to pull him to his feet.

"Hey," he protested, doing as she was urging but not sure why. "Who put you in charge?"

She smiled at him. He was like a big old sleepy bear, grumpy but amenable.

"I did," she said. "I've got everything organized. You don't have to worry about anything. Just come on over to my place and get all the sleep you can so you can shake this thing."

He was on his feet, but still looking befuddled. He swayed like a palm in the wind, and she jumped forward to prop him up and keep him from landing back on the bed.

He looked down at her, at where she held him, her arms around his chest and back, and he frowned.

"I will handle this," he muttered. "I'm in control."

She shook her head at him firmly. "You can't even control your eyelids, buster. Make way. I'm taking over."

And she began to lead him out of the room. They went along well enough, with her steering and him trying not to lean on her too heavily. They went through the living room and he waved at their guest.

"Hi, Mrs. Lark," he said. "I'm going over to sleep at J.J.'s." He shrugged and managed a smile. "Go figure."

J.J. peeked at the woman from around his back. She'd jumped up to see if she could help but now was hanging back, looking startled, and J.J. wanted to reassure her that this really wasn't as weird as it looked.

"I'll be right back, Mrs. Lark. Thank you so much."

Mrs. Lark frowned worriedly. "All right, dear. Is he...? Can you handle him?"

For some reason, that made J.J. laugh low in her throat. "Oh yes, I think I can handle him."

"She's one of those new take-charge women," Jack warbled, looking back at Mrs. Lark as they left the room. "She's going to organize my life."

J.J. suppressed a smile and hustled him through the cool midnight air and into her place. "Come on," she urged as he stopped and looked around. "Let's get you to bed."

He turned his bloodshot gaze on her in wonder. "I am dreaming, aren't I?"

She couldn't help but laugh. Even sick, he was good-natured and funny. His plight was bringing out mothering instincts she hadn't known she had, and she wanted to tuck him in and give him cool drinks and...*oh, give it up, J.J.!* What she really wanted to do was cuddle him until he felt much, much better. But that wasn't what was going to happen here.

She helped him up the stairs to her bedroom. He was awfully big and awkward to maneuver, but she did it. The covers were still pulled back from when she had leapt out and pulled on her clothes to see what was happening next door. It seemed hours ago now. But it couldn't have been more than forty-five minutes at the most.

"Come on," she said, stopping him from flopping down onto the bed. "Let's get your clothes off first."

He tried to help, but his fingers wouldn't work very well and he seemed so groggy. She got the buttons on his shirt, peeling it away from his gorgeous muscles and holding her breath while she did so. She hadn't realized this was going to be hazardous duty, but her heart was pounding as though she were in mortal danger.

She looked at the buckle of his belt and her nerve almost failed her. Was she really going to be able to do this?

"Hold still," she told him. "Just let me loosen this."

That was all she was going to do, just loosen the belt around his waist, push him back onto the bed and pull off his shoes, then cover him up and leave him alone. But once she unbuckled the belt, he reached down himself and undid his slacks, and before she knew it, they were sliding down toward the floor.

"Oh my," she whispered to herself, breathing quickly.

Well, this was exciting. Stimulating, in fact. She knew he was sick as a dog, but he still looked awfully good, and felt like velvet over steel, and she couldn't help but react. Just to have him here, to be doing this.

Suddenly something changed, like a shift in the wind. His large hands took hold of her shoulders and she looked up, shocked to find his gaze was dark as coal, smoldering. She gasped and he pulled her to him, raising her to her tiptoes. His body was burning, but by now, so was hers. Together, they fell to the bed, bodies entwined. His hand found her breast and his mouth settled on her collarbone, dropping hot kisses that sizzled on her skin. She writhed, her soul suggesting instant surrender in a despicable way she wasn't used to. She didn't do these things, especially not with a very sick man who needed rest.

But he felt so good.

Her hand trailed across the muscles of his arm. She'd never felt a man who was so hard, so solid. Why did that excite her? She didn't know. It had to be something in the primeval development, the inner antecedents of the soul. Regardless, it sent her senses spinning and she knew she wanted to be possessed by this man and no other.

"What?" She said the word aloud, her eyes popping open and staring into the night. What the hell had she just let her mind say? What the hell was she doing here?

"No," she said, pulling away and straightening her clothes, her cheeks flaming. "No, Jack."

He blinked up at her with a bewildered look. "No?"

"No." Still, she couldn't resist putting a hand on his forehead in a quick caress. "No, we can't do this."

"I'm sorry," he said in a sigh, lying back and closing his eyes. "I'm a jerk."

"No, not at all." She was touching him again, running a hand over his cheek. Why couldn't she stop doing this?

"You are sick and overmedicated and you don't know what you're doing."

She began tugging on the covers he'd scrambled, trying to get enough to cover him. His eyes opened again and he stared at her solemnly while she struggled with the covers and worked at tucking him in.

"That's where you're wrong, J.J.," he said, his voice a low and sexy rumble. "I'll have you know that I know exactly what I'm doing."

She hesitated, still leaning over him, and something in her wanted to laugh. "Then I guess you should be ashamed of yourself after all."

He smiled and his eyes closed again. "Oh, I see. You were just trying to give me an out, weren't you?"

She shook her head, smiling down at where he lay. He was irrepressible.

"I'm just trying to get you well," she told him, swallowing hard to fight back all the other urges that were fighting for release in her. "Sleep. I'll come back and check on you in the morning. And the phone is right here in case you need to call me. You know where I'll be."

He frowned like one not clear on the concept. "Where?"

She gazed down at him, her exasperation laced with laughter. "Next door. At your number."

"Oh. Of course." He looked up at her, pure longing in his blue eyes. "Why don't you just stay here and take care of me? Mrs. Lark can stay with the kids and—"

"No." She shivered, knowing how close she was to succumbing to that very temptation, but also knowing how disastrous such a decision would be. "You need peace and quiet. I'm going."

He shrugged, lying back and pulling the covers higher under his chin. "Whatever you say, Captain," he murmured.

She smiled and resisted one last touch. "Okay, plebe. Do as you're told."

"Aye-aye."

She slipped down the stairs, a smile on her face. She wasn't sure why she felt so happy, but she couldn't help it. He was a charming man and she'd definitely been charmed by him. But she didn't care. It was wonderful.

Seven

The children were still asleep when J.J. got back, and Mrs. Lark was beginning to doze, as well. J.J. sent her home with much appreciation and settled on the couch for what was left of the night. Luckily it was dawn before any of the babies stirred.

Baby Mack was the first to wake. She slipped in and brought him out into the living room without waking any of the others. He stared up at her, his eyes like blue stones, but he didn't make a sound. She smiled at him, but he didn't smile back, and she had the impression he was scoping her out, trying to decide if she was worth the effort or whether he should start screaming bloody murder.

He gave her a grace period. She changed him into fresh, fluffy diapers and a clean set of pajamas, and he lay quietly, watching her while she hummed a little tune to him. When she pulled him up to stand, he set his little feet squarely on the floor and tottered while she barely held his fingers, letting him test his balance.

"Baby Mack is going to be walking soon," she crooned to him. "And then we're all going to have to head for the hills."

She gave him a playful poke in his belly, but he frowned and she didn't try that again. "Are you hungry?" she asked him, picking up an empty bottle and waving it at him.

He crowed and lunged at it, so she figured that meant yes! and went quickly to the kitchen to fix him some milk. He followed, crawling high on his toes, moving in a sort of sideways crablike scramble faster than she could on her two feet.

She wasn't sure whether or not he needed warm milk and there was no one to ask. As luck would have it, the telephone rang at that very opportune moment, and when she lifted the receiver, she found Jack on the other end of the line.

"How are the kids?" he asked directly.

She smiled. His image had certainly changed in her eyes. The playboy was morphing into Daddy of the Year—at least when his kids were involved. "They're just fine," she reassured him. "You stay right where you are."

His voice was still rough with illness. "I don't know, J.J. I appreciate what you're doing and all. But I should be taking care of my own kids."

"You're sick," she said firmly. "Do you want them to get sick, too? They're doing just fine. You stay in bed."

"All right," he allowed reluctantly. "I don't want to chance them getting sick. I guess I can stay away from them for a little while."

"I tell you what," she offered. "Tell me where I can find the name of your doctor. We'll see if we can get a second opinion."

He gave her the name and told her where to look for certain other items. And then, sounding tired, he started to say goodbye. "You're sure everything's going okay?"

"Oh, yes."

"You don't need anything?"

Baby Mack threw a toy across the room at that very moment, which reminded her. She hesitated. "Well, just one little thing."

"What's that?"

"Do you warm the babies' milk before you give them their bottles?"

He laughed roughly. "Oh, Lord, I keep forgetting how little you know! I'd better come on over—"

"Don't you dare! Just tell me. I may not know much about babies, but I can learn."

He sighed. "Okay. Okay. Do you warm their milk? Yes, but not a lot. Just to take the chill off it. And if they want to drink out of those little cups with the spouts, I usually leave it cold."

"Thank you." And she hung up before he had time to think twice.

She settled Baby Mack on the couch with his bottle, then went in to check on the girls. They were still sleeping, like twin dolls with round cheeks and curling blond hair. She stood and watched them for a few minutes, unable to turn away. What had she called them the other day? Little monsters? No way. These were angels. It was written all over them.

When she came back out, she found that Baby Mack had abandoned his bottle and crawled across the floor to a plastic play guitar that had been left in the corner. He was plucking the strings and emitting strange sounds out of his mouth. She stopped, staring at him, wondering what in the world he was doing, and suddenly she realized what it was. He thought he was singing.

"Going to take after your dad, are you?" she asked him, laughing.

She sat down on the couch and watched him. He was so cute, but he didn't look a thing like his father, not the way Annie did. They were all so cute. Four children. The concept was frightening.

Jack was an amazing man. The more she got to know the situation, the more she had to be impressed by his devotion to these kids. How many men would do something like this? She had to admit it. He was a pretty special guy.

Parts of her tingled with excitement when she thought of going back over to check on him. She'd been thinking off and on for hours about what had happened between them the night before, about how she felt about it.

It was humiliating to admit how much she was attracted to him. Because despite everything, the Good Daddy award and all, he was still a man who seemed to have some sort of relationship with every woman who came into his life. Did she really want to stand in a line behind Bambi and Marguerite? Ha! No way.

This time it was daylight and she was going to keep control of her impulses.

Baby Mack came back to his bottle and started to doze, and she rested, knowing she was going to need any energy she could store up. Kristi and Kathy woke about a half hour later, and J.J. was just about hitting hysteria when Annie finally got up and started to help her a little. Once she got a moment's peace, she called the doctor and was shocked to find the man ready to run on over and check in on everyone at the drop of a hat.

"Jack is a good friend of mine," the doctor told her. "He's a great guy, you know. I owe him. In fact, I wouldn't have been able to finish medical school if it weren't for the money he loaned me at the time. I'll be right over."

He turned out to be young but compassionate and the babies squealed happily when he tickled them and Annie laughed at his jokes. Mrs. Lark also stopped by and J.J. took the opportunity to run next door and see if things were ready for the doctor over there. She called out as she came into her condo, then climbed the stairs and found Jack still in bed but looking a little more alert.

"The doctor is checking out Annie and the babies," she told him, her gaze hitting him and sliding away. Despite the fact that she'd helped undress him, the sight of his naked chest sent her heart into a faster cadence. "He'll be over here in a few minutes."

"Shoot. No time for a quick affair then, is there?"

She didn't dignify that with a response, though she had to stifle a smile. She glanced at his face and felt a glow of relief. He actually appeared lucid today. Surely he was getting better.

Then she looked at the state of her bedroom and frowned.

"What's going on here?" she said as she noted that her little clock radio was lying on its head on the ground.

He looked sheepish. "Oh, yeah. I was reaching for the phone and the radio went flying. I forgot to pick it up again. I hope I didn't break it."

She bent down to retrieve it and noted the cord had come out of the wall plug. Sighing, she bent down to fix it.

Leaning over the edge of the bed, he watched her with interest. "How are my babies?" he asked.

"Fine," she told him, looking up and realizing their noses were almost touching. Quickly she looked down again. "You can ask the doctor for any details you need in a few minutes." She frowned, unable to get the plug into the socket correctly for some reason. "Darn," she said under her breath.

"Sorry," he said again.

This time she didn't say it was all right. She knew why she was all thumbs and she really didn't want to go into it.

"Oh, by the way," Jack mentioned casually, when she didn't reply, "some guy called you this morning."

If she'd been paying closer attention, she might have noticed the twinkle in his eyes. But she was bent over, fixing the plug in the wall, and she didn't see it. Finally the plug went in the way it was supposed to and she felt a small flash of triumph.

"What guy?" she said, finishing up and straightening, and not paying too much attention as yet. The bedside table had to be moved back in front of the wall plug and she began edging it over.

Jack raised his eyebrows, leaning against his pillows and enjoying this to the hilt. "He said his name was Martin something."

She whirled on her heel and looked at him, hard. Now the twinkle was plain to see and that made her very uneasy. "Martin? What did he say, exactly?"

His eyes narrowed as though he'd caught her in something secret. "Ah, you want the exact words, do you?"

Giving him an exasperated look, she went back to moving furniture. "Yes. Please."

He was working hard at driving her crazy and she knew it. Was she going to let him get her goat? She glanced at him out of the corner of her eye and had to suppress a smile. He was being awfully engaging for a sick man. There was something about him in this state that appealed to something in her, and she didn't think it was her nursing instincts. In fact, she had to restrain herself from touching him again, putting a hand on his forehead, adjusting his covers. No, he was too alert now to go back to those tactics.

"The words?" she reminded him.

He considered. "I think he said, 'Is this J.J.'s?'"

"And you said?" she prodded impatiently, putting back the radio and standing aside to look at her handiwork with satisfaction.

"I said yes."

She turned and looked at him, then gave an aggravated moan and waved her hands in the air. He was bound and determined to mine this for all it was worth, wasn't he?

"And then he said..." she prompted expectantly, as though drawing out a child.

Jack was unconcerned about her impatience. He cocked his head to the side as though trying to remember exactly. "I think he said, 'Is she there?'"

She sank to sit beside him on the bed. There didn't seem to be any use in hurrying. Why did you always have to take men by the hand and lead them through these things? You had to drag the pertinent information out of them every time. She folded her hands and waited, but finally she couldn't stand it any longer.

"And then, what did you say?" she coaxed. "After he said, 'Is she there?'" she added, just in case he'd forgotten.

His handsome face was the picture of radiant innocence. It was the look of an angel, a naive and misunderstood saint—a man who could do no wrong, not even if tempted by cash.

"I said, 'I don't know. I just woke up and she's not here in the bed. Would you like me to go out and see if she's downstairs?'"

She stared at him for a long moment, her heart thudding in her chest, her outrage growing. Maybe he was merely tormenting her. Had to be. Oh, yes, had to be. That smug look on his face had to be a bluff.

"You didn't," she said firmly at last. There might even have been a touch of menace in her tone.

He smiled at her, seemingly pleased with her reaction. "I might have. I can't really remember it word for word." His eyebrows raised as though he'd had a sudden idea. "I guess we'll have to ask Martin."

"Oh!" She could cheerfully have strangled him at this point, and actually made a move toward his throat, but it really wasn't proper to cut off the wind supply to a sick man, so she resisted. "I know you couldn't have said any such thing," she stated, keeping her annoyance with him out of her voice, but not out of the flash of her eyes.

Noting the evidence of her wrath, he tried to keep the corners of his mouth from twitching, but he wasn't very successful.

"So who is this Martin, anyway?" he asked, as though supremely unconcerned about the topic. "That macho sportscaster on your station?"

She tapped her foot. She'd never tapped her foot at a man before in her life, but she did it now, and with gusto. "I don't have to go into this with you," she said warningly. "It's really none of your business."

He nodded his satisfaction. "I thought it was him. He's not your type, you know."

"Is that right?" She fluffed up his pillow rather more vigorously than was necessary but resisted the impulse to dump it on his face. Instead, she started for the doorway, deciding it might be the better part of valor to get out while she still hadn't committed a murder.

"I suppose you're an expert on these things," she said crisply as she went.

"Of course."

She stopped. She couldn't resist. Looking back, she asked, "Then, just what is my type?"

He frowned, looking her up and down. "I see you with a tall guy, sort of handsome, very strong, quiet, cool, collected. A guy—" he threw out his hands as though it were a matter of course "—sort of like me."

She couldn't help it. She burst out laughing.

"That'll be the day!" she cried as she started off down the stairs. "You get some more sleep. I'll check in on you again at lunchtime."

"Hurry back," he called in a forlorn voice, but she was already out the door.

And she laughed softly all the way back to the other condo, even while she worried. What was it about Jack Remington that seemed to get to her emotions, either anger or laughter, so easily? She'd never known another man like Jack. He was unique. And she was very much afraid she was beginning to like him a little bit too much.

The doctor said the babies looked fine so far, but Jack was a mess.

"His throat is a hotbed of massive infection," he told J.J. "He'd better stay away from the children for another twenty-four hours. Call me if the babies show any symptoms."

J.J. nodded, but she hardly had time to think about anything but keeping the babies warm and dry and clean and full of food. There was never a dull moment. Concentrate on one child and the other two were getting into mischief somewhere. She began to feel like a circus clown who kept putting away dogs that kept popping out in new places and never stayed put.

And then there was Gregor. She hadn't met the cat before, but she did now. Gregor was shy and didn't come out much, except when he was hungry, and then he was a major pest, meowing and rubbing against her ankles until she got his food set out for him. A quick meal and he was back in hiding somewhere in the condo, and the babies spent hours looking for him.

"Ga-ga," Baby Mack would call, stooping to look under the couch. "Ga-ga!"

But Gregor was too wise to answer.

At one point in the morning, J.J. sat Annie down in front of the Saturday morning cartoons on the television, surfing channels until she found one that wasn't too ugly and hard edged.

"Good grief. What kind of kids watch these mean shows?" she asked the little girl as she searched.

"Mean kids," Annie replied, and J.J. thought she was probably right.

She finally got the babies down for a late-morning nap and had to decide between sitting down to rest and running over to see how Jack was doing. She didn't think long. Despite her exhaustion, Jack won out.

She went in quietly this time, warned by some stray bit of feminine intuition that he would be sleeping. And he was. She crept quietly into the room and looked at him, knowing it wasn't fair to watch him when he was so unprotected. But this way she actually got to look at him. When he was awake, he spent most of the time dueling with verbal jabs and she hardly had time to think, much less look.

So now she looked. Asleep, he had a younger appearance and it reminded her of the old days in Sacramento. When she let herself remember how it had really been, she knew she'd had a raging crush on him. That was why it had hurt so much when he'd criticized her work. And then when he'd had her fired . . .

But that was long ago. She didn't want to bring up all the old bitterness, the old pain. She hadn't let it hold her back then and she wasn't going to let it trip her up now. Jack Remington was just a man. And she was a woman with a career and an ambition she was still dedicated to.

"So watch out, J.J.," she told herself as she turned to go back to the kids. "Just watch yourself."

Jack clicked off the television and stared at the wall. This recuperating stuff was getting old. He wanted to get back to his kids. He had to admit he'd needed the rest, but now he was saturated with it. He had to get back into the swing or he'd forget how it was done.

His kids—that was what life was all about now. Leaving them alone with strangers was not a good thing to do, and being away from them just emphasized in his mind how big a part of his life they were. Now that he could think more clearly and go over the facts in his head, he knew it was time to listen to those other voices—the voices of so-called reason, the voices of negativity. He had to face the fact that they might be right. It was just possible he really couldn't do this alone. Maybe he really couldn't make it.

After all, when he'd come down with the flu, he'd needed others to step in and take over for him. He'd sworn up and down ever since he'd brought the babies home from the hospital that he would be able to do it all alone. And he'd been wrong in this instance. How did he know that it wouldn't happen again?

Suddenly his mind was full of Phoebe, her look, her scent, her anger—and he felt a revulsion such as he hadn't felt since she'd died. This was all her fault, after all. If she hadn't become pregnant, thinking that was how she would be able to hold him, if she hadn't had the triplets, if she hadn't died . . .

He writhed on the bed, hating himself for feeling this way, hating Phoebe, hating everything. Everything but those beautiful babies, those three little personalities who hadn't asked to be born, who now asked for nothing but love and nourishment. And that he would give them. That at the very least.

No, he wasn't going to give up. He was going to raise his children. No one else could do it the way he could. No one else could possibly love them the way he did. No one else was their father. No matter what he had to give up to do it, it had to be done, and it would be.

Getting up, he took a shower, feeling refreshed and almost normal when he was done. He itched to go over and see his children, but he knew he had to wait. Cocking his head, he listened at the common wall, but he couldn't hear any crying. J.J. was doing a good job with them.

He smiled, thinking of her. What a breath of fresh air she was. Too bad she was intent upon making it in television. If she wasn't so ambitious, he might have been able to talk her into taking over Marguerite's job after all. The thought of his children being raised by sunny J.J. instead of dour Marguerite set up a longing in him. If only...

And yet, he knew that would never work. The longings J.J. set off in him were as much on the physical side as on the side of child development. He'd been without a woman to love and make love with for much too long, but those were the breaks and he was going to go on missing that aspect of life until these kids were raised. That was all there was to it.

"So dream on, Jack," he told himself with some sarcasm. "Dreams are all you're going to get."

Eight

———

J.J. came back later that evening to see how Jack was doing, bringing him soup. And though at first he refused it, making a face, she set the bowl next to the bed and eventually he relented. The aroma got to him and he had to try it.

She smiled and felt very good about her efforts. It had come out of a package, but she had mixed it together herself. Maybe there was hope of learning to cook.

She watched as he slowly spooned soup into his mouth, watched the way his arm flexed, the shadow of his unshaven beard on his handsome face.

Watch it, she warned herself. *Don't get carried away.*

She supervised, coaxing him to finish it all, and while he ate, she told him stories about funny things Baby Mack had done and how Kathy had almost pulled a chair over on herself and how adorable Annie had been when she'd helped make the dinner.

"I fixed them peas and carrots and hamburgers," she told him. "But without the buns. So we used slices of bread. They loved it."

Another success, and she glowed as she told him about it.

The soup seemed to revive his energy level. He put down the bowl and favored her with a mischievous smile.

"Look what I've got," he told her, reaching behind the bed and pulling out a large book. "I found your scrapbook."

She laughed, shaking her head, coloring slightly. "How did you find that?"

"I looked through all the bookcases until I found where you had it. I knew you'd have one."

She laughed again, tempted to put her hands to her face in embarrassment, but she couldn't help but be pleased. Her scrapbook was the story of her life. People usually ran in the opposite direction when she pulled it out to show them, and here Jack was interested.

He began leafing through it, turning the large pages and looking at each picture, each clipping, in turn. "You moved all the way from . . . looks like California, according to this. And you brought hardly a piece of anything with you other than your clothes." He grinned at her. "And still, you brought your scrapbook."

"I . . ." she began, but he shook his head, ready with his own explanation.

"I knew you would. People like us, who work in a business where there are an awful lot of jerks who make it their life's work to destroy you in any way they can, we sometimes need a strong support system." He hefted the scrapbook up with one hand. "And this is the best thing going. Notices. Things you can look back at to prove to yourself that someone thought you were pretty good at something."

To J.J.'s surprise, a lump rose in her throat and emotion prickled at her eyelids. "People like us." Had he really said that? For just a moment, she felt such a sense of connection with this man that she had to hold herself back from reaching for him.

He looked up but didn't seem to notice. "I've watched you doing the news," he noted. "I've watched you every day."

"Oh, you have?"

She waited, knowing what had to come next. You didn't throw out a comment like that and then not tell someone how much you liked their work. It just wasn't done. He had to tell her how wonderful she was. It didn't matter what he really thought. He had to say it. It went with the territory.

But he didn't say a word. He kept leafing through the scrapbook and stopped to smile at a picture here, an article there, but he didn't say a word.

"I've sure worked at enough stations," she said, giving him another chance, in case it was just a matter of his having forgotten. She looked up and smiled at him.

"That you have," he noted. "I think you've worked at more than I have. You've had a lot of experience." He went on looking, and he didn't give her one scrap of praise.

She was itching to say something, itching to ask him what he thought. Why didn't he say it? Why couldn't he just say something innocuous, like, "You look great against blue backgrounds" or "I like the way you pause just before you begin a new topic." Anything, at this point, would be better than this deafening silence.

Then he raised his head and met her gaze, moving so suddenly she was startled.

"So where's this career of yours headed, J.J.? What's your goal?" He watched her carefully, as though her answer mattered to him.

She sat up a little straighter. "Well, what do you think?" She gave a casual shrug, the sort of move she would make when talking of this with anyone else in the business. "New York, of course," she said glibly. "The networks."

He stared at her for a long moment, and she wished she hadn't said it quite that superficially.

But he surprised her again. "I remember when that was my goal," he said quietly at last.

"What happened?" she asked, her curiosity superseding everything else. She really wanted to know. "Why isn't it your goal anymore?"

He smiled and didn't answer, going back to her scrapbook. She watched him turn pages, and she swallowed her frustration with the man. There were some things he just wasn't going to tell her, weren't there? She supposed she was going to have to accept that, no matter how annoying it was. She sighed and shook her head.

Then she remembered that she had another reason for being there at the moment. She'd chided herself for not doing this sooner. It was really far past time to hand over the letter she'd found in the entryway of her condo.

Rising and going to a drawer in her dresser, she withdrew the letter and held it out to him.

"What's that?" he said, putting aside the scrapbook but not offering to take the envelope from her, looking at it suspiciously.

"A letter." She waved it at him. "Smell the perfume?" she asked, although she didn't smell anything herself, and after all this time, any scent that had been put on the envelope was surely evaporated.

"Who's it for?" he asked, still not trusting it.

She drew it back, getting annoyed with his hesitancy. "You."

"A letter for me?" He frowned and pulled the covers up over his chest, turning onto his elbow. "Who's it from?"

She shrugged and glanced at him sideways. "Bambi, I imagine."

His face changed dramatically. "What are you talking about?" He frowned, studying what he could see of the envelope she still held in her hand. "There's no stamp, no address."

"That's right," she said, frowning as she tried to read something into his reactions. He was certainly reacting. But what did it mean? "It was left here, in this condo. I found it. It seems to have slipped down behind the hallway table at some point."

He searched her face and she began to enjoy this more than she'd thought she would. He really didn't trust her and two could play this teasing game. What did he think, that she'd made this up? Well, let him stew a while longer. She merely smiled and waited for him to get curious enough to demand to see it.

"How do you know it's for me?" he asked, still wary, his blue eyes clouded with suspicion.

"It says so, right here on the envelope." She waved it in the air again. Time to put on a little more pressure. "It's probably a love letter, don't you think?" she said coolly, watching his face closely.

He laughed shortly, looking incredulous. "I doubt it."

She cocked her head to the side, watching him through narrowed eyes. "Or maybe a letter to tell you where to reach her. Where to meet."

He stared at her for a moment, then shook his head as though he couldn't believe what he saw and heard.

"You grew up watching too much television, didn't you?" he said softly. "Or reading too many Nancy Drew mysteries."

She was growing impatient. She hadn't expected him to take this long to show interest. If he was playacting, he was awfully good at it. Could it be he really didn't care much, that he really had no romantic attachment to the woman? Or was he just about the coolest customer on record?

"Don't you want to read it?" she asked. "It might be important." She waited a moment, and when he didn't comment, added rather conspiratorially, leaning toward him and looking significant, "It might just change everything."

He laughed shortly, enjoying her machinations but not sure what she was trying to prove. "What could it possibly change?"

She shrugged, eyeing him speculatively. "Everything."

His mouth turned down at the corners, as though he were just too cynical to put up with much more of this.

"You said that, but I'm still not convinced."

She sighed impatiently. "You'll never know until you read it. And what you read—"

"May change my life. Yes, I get the picture." He laughed again, his blue eyes sparkling as he looked at her. "Oh, you romantic, you." He held out his hand. "Here. Give me the letter. Let's go ahead and take that step into the unknown. Let destiny have her way with us."

She liked the way he said "us," but she had a feeling it didn't really mean anything. Still, it sounded nice.

"Here's the letter." She handed it to him. "Do you want me to leave the room while you . . . ?"

He gave her a baleful look and ripped open the envelope, quickly skimming the contents. Then he looked up, looked right into her eyes, and nodded slowly.

"Well, you were right," he said solemnly. "This really does change everything."

She blanched and clasped her fingers together nervously. "What do you mean?" she asked him, wondering if she really wanted to know.

"Bambi..." He hesitated and licked his lower lip, as though not sure how to tell her. Then his gaze held hers again.

"Bambi has made me a proposition. It's a serious step and I'm going to have to think about it very carefully." He looked at her, searching her eyes, her face. "It's going to take some thought. It's a very personal matter, and because it's so personal, she put it in writing before she left, she says, so that I could go ahead and turn her down without being afraid of hurting her feelings to her face, in case I don't want to do it."

J.J. could hardly breathe now. She regretted that she hadn't destroyed the darn thing on sight. This was awful. She was feeling sick. Well, maybe not sick exactly. But it was darn irritating. That woman was becoming more and more unappealing all the time.

"What is it?" she asked him softly, her eyes huge, and she was dreading the answer.

He stared at her as the seconds ticked by, then nodded at her and said, "Come here and I'll tell you."

Her eyes widened. What was this, just a ploy? "Oh no," she said, shaking her head despite the fact that her pulse had made a tingling surge at his suggestion. "You tell me from there."

He shrugged, folding the paper back into the envelope and waiting a moment before he said, "Are you ready? Are you sure you're okay with this? Because I don't want to shock you."

She bit her lip, feeling as though she were about to explode. "Just tell me, please," she said in a voice trembling with anticipation of disaster.

He waited another moment, then grimaced. "Well, I don't know. It is awfully personal and—"

With a cry of rage, she came at him with a pillow and he laughed, ducking away, while she pummeled him for a brief moment, then flew back to her chair and out of reach.

"Okay, okay," he said, still chuckling. "Here it is. Bambi has asked me . . . to be the godfather of her first child."

She blinked and frowned. What? Had she heard that wrong? Not the father? No. He had said something else. "The godfather?" she repeated dully.

"Yes." He grinned at her. "Oh, didn't I tell you she married Hank Garbon, the station sales rep? It was a tiny wedding, just before the justice of the peace. She was working as an outside saleswoman, but she'd come here as one of the station vice president's girlfriends, so feelings were running high when she fell in love with someone else." He grinned, remembering.

"They didn't invite anyone from the station to the wedding. I was best man. Bambi and I got to be good friends because she found she could cry on my shoulder, and knowing the people she was involved with, I understood. Hank is a good guy. They moved to New Mexico. And before she left, I guess she wrote this letter and meant to bring it over with a stack of papers she left with me when she went. It must have fallen behind the table at that time."

J.J. was still having trouble assimilating all this. "When was that?" she asked.

"About three weeks ago. She probably wonders why I haven't written. I'd better get back to her right away."

J.J. sat and stared at him. She felt like a balloon after all the air had escaped in one long whistling whoosh. He had played with her like a cat played with a mouse. She should hate him. So why did she have this irresistible urge to laugh aloud? Why did she want so badly to go to him and touch his face and lie beside him on that bed and...

She shook her head to clear it. None of that. Things had to be kept in their proper perspective, and it was time she got back to the babies.

"I'd better go," she said abruptly, rising and looking down at him. "Anything I can get you before I leave?"

He gazed at her steadily for a moment. "Remember when you brought me here last night?" he asked her.

She flushed. That was something she had hoped he wouldn't remember. Neither one of them had been thinking too clearly at the time.

"No," she said quickly. "And anyway, it didn't happen."

He laughed, throwing back his head and letting the laughter spill out, and she turned and dashed for the stairs. There was no way she was going to hang around to be tempted by him any longer. A man who could act the way he did—was just about the most attractive sort of man she'd ever known.

Mrs. Lark had been sitting with the children and she stayed awhile longer, helping J.J. put them down for the night. It had been a long, exhausting day, but J.J. was feeling a sense of happiness that she couldn't explain. It had something to do with Jack, but it also had something to do with these babies and Annie. Just being with them, seeing them through their day, had been a joy to her in a way she would never have expected. She could hardly believe it. She was having a wonderful time.

Mrs. Lark noted it herself, smiling and patting her arm and telling her how well she seemed to relate to the children. But then she had a word of warning.

"Be careful, my dear," she said, making sure Annie was out of earshot before she spoke. "It only takes a few hours to bond with a baby."

"Bond with a baby?" J.J. wasn't sure just what she meant.

She nodded wisely. "I know all about it. I once tried to adopt a sweet little girl. Angelique was her name." A far-away look crept into her hazel eyes. "I had her for three days and then the mother changed her mind and took her back." She shook her head, the sadness real to her again. "When they came and took her away from me, I thought they might as well take my heart, too. I cried for days, weeks. Even now I feel a pain in my heart where that child once was."

"After only three days?" J.J. murmured, thinking about how close she had become to these babies, and how quickly.

Mrs. Lark nodded. "Oh, yes, my dear. It takes no time at all with a baby. That is the special gift they have. It's an element of survival for them, I suppose."

The kindly lady left, but her words echoed in J.J.'s head. She peeked in at the babies. They had gone down so easily tonight, and they were all three sleeping soundly. She tip-toed past their cribs, looking at each in turn. What beautiful children they were. There were none others like them.

Would she ever have babies like this? For the first time in her life, it seemed almost possible.

The night was still young as far as Annie was concerned, and when J.J. came out of the babies' room, she talked her into playing a board game with her, then reading her a story, and finally the yawns began to come.

"Time for bed, sleepyhead," J.J. told her tenderly, leading her to her room.

The first thing that struck her as she entered was the picture of a beautiful woman on Annie's nightstand. The woman was laughing, her blue eyes full of a wildness, an abandon, that looked almost startling. She had the tilt of the head, the air, the confidence, of a movie star. And yet there was something a little disturbing in her face.

"Is that your mother, Annie?" she asked.

Annie nodded.

"She's so beautiful," J.J. noted.

"I don't look like her," Annie told her matter-of-factly. "I look like my daddy."

"And you are very beautiful, too," J.J. told her, handing her a clean nightgown.

"Thank you," Annie said, as though that were a matter of course. "Will you help me say my prayers?"

Annie prayed for protection for her Daddy and for J.J. and for Marguerite, and for numerous other people J.J. had never heard of. Then she climbed into bed and J.J. leaned down to kiss her good-night.

"Will you take me to the park one of these days?" Annie asked her solemnly.

J.J. stuck out a hand to shake as a bargain. "I'll do that," she promised. "You and me, to the park."

"Good." Annie snuggled down in her covers. "I hope my daddy comes home tomorrow," she said, half talking, half yawning.

"I'm sure he will, darling. Good night."

They had a pretty calm night. Baby Mack woke up twice, and at two in the morning, he wanted to play, cooing and crawling off to make her chase him. But she finally got him settled back down. And then she couldn't sleep herself. She spent a lot of time thinking about that picture in Annie's room.

What did she know, after all, about this family and its relationships? She felt as though she knew Jack because she'd known him from way-back-when, but she really didn't know him at all. She had no idea what had happened to him in the years since then, where these children had come from, what had happened with the woman he'd been married to.

She had better tread lightly here, she decided. Because, not knowing the background of this family, how was she going to know when she was making a false move? There were things she was going to need to find out about.

In the meantime, she was taking care of four children. Four! That number boggled her mind. And yet, she was doing it. And caring a bit for a sick man on the side.

Caring a little too much, she might say. And that would have to stop soon. Because work came first. That was the way it had always been, and the way it would always be. No waffling on commitments.

But she had to admit, all this ambition made for a pretty lonely life. So she was glad for this respite, this time with the Remington family. Actually she was piling up memories she would always cherish.

"Think of it that way," she told herself. "And don't think so much about Jack."

Morning came and so did the babies. They woke at the crack of dawn, ready to scramble around and squeal with delight and get into everything. J.J. dragged herself out of bed and made some coffee, and before she knew it, she was raring to go, as well, chasing after babies, making bottles, changing diapers, as though she'd been doing it all her life.

The doctor called to say he would be back in the afternoon to check things out and give the word on whether Jack was well enough to move back in with his children. J.J. began planning what the babies would wear to greet him, going through their clothes and finding the most adorable outfits she could.

At one point, halfway into their morning, the telephone rang again. J.J. was in the middle of giving Kristi a bath and she knew better than to leave her alone, even for an instant.

"Can you get that, Annie?" she called, thinking it was probably Jack on the line.

She heard the patter of Annie's little feet as she ran for it. Kristi began playing pat-a-cake with the water, spreading droplets everywhere, and J.J. laughed, making Kristi laugh along with her. Out of nowhere came the urge to hug and kiss the beautiful child and she did it, her heart overflowing. This was what it felt like to love a baby, wasn't it? Wow. Pretty neat.

Suddenly Annie was running toward the bathroom. "Guess what?" she cried. "Marguerite's all better and she's coming back. She says today."

J.J.'s laughter froze on her face and her heart sank. "Marguerite?" she repeated. "Oh, that's nice."

But the joy had gone out of the moment. She pulled Kristi out of the tub and began drying her, but her mind was filled with regret. The idyll was over. She knew that instinctively. With Marguerite coming back, everything would change.

Don't be an idiot, she told herself fiercely. *There's no reason to be jealous of Marguerite.* But deep inside, she knew she was. And it wasn't because of Jack. It was because of the children.

Mrs. Lark spent Sunday morning at church, so there was no one to watch the babies and let J.J. run over and check on Jack. She called him, but somehow she never got around to telling him Marguerite was coming back. They spent the entire conversation talking about Kathy's tooth coming in and Baby Mack's attempt to say "Annie" that had ended up more like "Nnnugh." And then Jack had said he missed her.

Missed her. Of all the silly things to say. She held it tightly in her soul and savored it, even though she knew he was just getting bored and lonely and hadn't meant it at all. Had he?

And then Marguerite arrived.

By now, J.J. hadn't really been expecting the floozy she'd imagined when she'd first heard about the woman. Still, she was surprised at what she saw coming in the doorway, carrying two very used brown paper bags full of knitting and tissues and cold medicines. The woman's blond hair was flying about her face, probably the result of a very bad permanent wave. She wore a housedress that didn't leave a clue as to whether or not she might have a figure and was shuffling in shoes that looked suspiciously like carpet slippers. Sniffing loudly, she plopped the bags down onto the floor and stood looking at J.J.

"Yes?" she said sharply, as though J.J. had just knocked on her door and she wanted to know what she'd come for.

"Hi," J.J. said, trying to smile. "You must be Marguerite. I'm J. J. Jensen. I live in the condo next door and I've been—"

"Sorry, I have no time to chat," Marguerite said, dismissing her with a wave of her hand. "You better go on now. I got to get these babies back into shape."

J.J. blinked and tried again, forcing her smile but sincerely wanting to be friendly. "Oh, but you don't understand, I've been—"

"Yes, yes, I know already, Annie told me on the telephone. Thanks for all good things you did. You can go now. Marguerite is back." She frowned, as though J.J. were really a pain in the neck and she didn't care who knew it.

J.J. hadn't admitted to herself that things were over. She still was counting on logic to win Marguerite to her side when it was obvious pure spite and emotion were all that were going to count here.

"But you're going to need help with all these children," she noted sensibly, "at least until Jack is back."

The woman shook her head, her face stormy. "Marguerite can take care of it. I been doing it for months. Go on." She waved her hand as though shooing away a pesky dog. "You can go back to where you came from."

And she turned to stomp off into the babies' room, effectively wiping away the fact that J.J. had ever been there.

J.J. stood with her mouth open. It was pretty obvious the woman wanted her to disappear and never darken their doorway again, and her first impulse was to fight. These were her babies, damn it! She'd cared for them for almost two days now. Marguerite had no business shoving her aside this way.

But her cooler side prevailed. After all, she had been a pinch hitter, and pinch hitters didn't get to be in the starting lineup, did they? What she'd been doing here was play-acting, playing house. It was ridiculous to cling to it. It was time for her to admit it. This was over.

She heard Annie cry out with happiness to see her old friend back again, and she winced hearing it, as though Annie had turned against her.

Don't do this, she warned herself as she gathered her things and prepared to leave. *Don't make this a contest between the two of you.*

But she couldn't help it. Hearing Annie's affection for the other woman after Marguerite had treated J.J. with such hostility almost brought tears to her eyes. It was time for her to go. Things were getting back to normal. She wasn't needed any longer. Quietly she slipped out and walked in the sunny morning back to her own condo.

Nine

Jack was sitting at her breakfast bar looking remarkably well. His hair was still damp from a recent shower and he'd put on his slacks and a shirt, which was hanging open, revealing his tanned and sculptured chest. She paused for a split second as she came into the room, steeling herself not to react, and in doing so, of course, reacting all the more.

But he didn't seem to notice. He had the invitation to Sara's baby shower in his hand and he waved it at her.

"Your friend's shower is coming up," he noted. "Here's a coincidence. I'm planning to take the kids to Denver that same weekend, to visit my parents."

She glanced into his eyes, but they were bland and good-natured, not giving away any hint as to what he was thinking. Was he inviting her along with his brood? She hardly thought so. Then why had he brought it up?

"I don't think I'll be able to make it," she told him as she slid onto a bar stool opposite where he was sitting. "I'm scheduled to work that weekend."

He put the card down on the counter and looked at her levelly. "Get out of it," he said, as though that were the most sensible thing to do.

Her laugh was short and not very sweet. "I'm here pursuing a career, remember? In fact, my agent has informed me in so many words that this is probably my last chance."

He frowned, not liking the sense of discouragement he detected in her tone of voice.

"Your last chance at the networks?" he guessed astutely. "So what? You don't really want to end up there. Believe me, I've known people who have, and the toll it takes is incredible. Only the strong survive in that market."

She lifted her chin. Her mood wasn't very good to begin with, and she certainly wasn't going to take that comment lying down. "You don't think I'm strong enough?" she demanded.

He laughed, enjoying her defiant face. "I know you're strong, J.J. And talented. But why waste all your talents on that sort of life? It isn't worth it."

Wasn't it? She thought fleetingly of her own background, of the squalor she'd grown up in, of all her hard work to rise out of that situation, of how far she'd come. She thought of her college roommates, of the homes they'd come from, ranging from comfortable to privileged. That was all she'd ever wanted—to prove she was just as good, could live just as well. But how could she explain that to Jack?

"Tell me the truth," she said, her face impassive, her voice wooden. "You've seen me work. What do you think? Can I make it?"

He was silent for a long moment, as though trying to decide what to tell her, what she needed. And finally he spoke very quietly.

"I've seen you read the news and I've seen your investigative reporting. I've seen spots you've written yourself. You're very good, J.J. You could make it. You have all the skills, the talent, the looks, everything." He shrugged, looking troubled. "But I'm sure you know there are hundreds of people who have all that. There has to be another element."

She waited, heart beating. It was such a relief to know that he liked her work. For some reason, right now his opinion was all that mattered. But she was listening, waiting for the other shoe to fall. What was that other element that she might just lack?

"Luck," he told her softly. "Being in the right place at the right time. Or, best of all, you've got to know somebody."

Her heart sank. She'd known these things all along, she just hadn't completely faced them. "You've got to know somebody," she repeated, nodding. "Yes, I've certainly heard that before. You've got to know somebody. And I don't."

Jack's smile was slow and careful. "Yes, you do. You know me."

She gazed at him for a moment, shocked. Did Jack have ties that high up? Could he really pull strings at the network level?

And then she laughed. Oh. Of course. He was joking, wasn't he? After all, if he had ties that high, why hadn't he gone to work in New York himself?

"Very funny," she told him, shaking her head. "You had me going there for a minute."

He didn't say a word and she took a deep breath. His judgment on her abilities was gratifying, and it did help to lift her spirits, but the fact was, there was still a situation that had to be dealt with. And for some reason, that seemed to be overshadowing everything else for her today. She turned and looked at him for a long moment, then braced herself and told him what she should have said from the start.

"Marguerite's back," she informed him glumly, thinking he would see immediately what that meant—that she was through playing nanny.

"Is she?" He actually looked happy about it. "Oh, good. Then you can finally get some sleep."

"I don't want sleep," she said, though she knew she was being pouty and childish.

"You need sleep," he told her gently, reaching out to tilt her face up and inspect the dark circles under her eyes and then puzzling over the stormy, rebellious look in her gaze. "My children have been running you off your feet."

His fingers felt electric on her chin line and she wanted to lean toward him. Everything in her was yearning for... something.

"I can't tell you how much I appreciate all you've done," he said.

"Don't," she said fiercely, pulling away from his touch. "Don't waste your appreciation on me," she added, turning and sliding off the bar stool to stomp into the kitchen. "I enjoyed every minute of it."

He slid off his seat and came toward her, frowning slightly. "What's the matter?" he asked as he took her by the elbow, pulling her around to face him. She stared up at him, her pulse fluttering in her throat.

"I guess you'll be going back to the way life was before... before..." She shook her head, unable to express it in words, but the fear trembled in her voice.

His hand tightened on her arm and something just as elemental began to beat in the pit of his stomach.

"Of course not," he said, managing to keep his voice light and smooth. "J.J., how can I go back to the way I was before I knew you? You're not that easy to forget."

Turning to look at him, she hesitated, then began to laugh softly. "You want to bet?" she challenged. "You've already forgotten me once."

His head went back and his eyes narrowed. "What are you talking about?"

She blinked up at him. "We've met before." Quickly she recounted the bare bones of their past association. "You even had me fired," she told him. "You don't remember that?"

He frowned, completely at sea. "Had you fired? Why?"

She shrugged and told him about the newsbreak she'd flubbed.

Before she'd finished talking, he was already shaking his head. "Now *that* I deny," he said firmly. "I don't remember ever having anyone fired. What do you think I am, J.J.? I was a beginner once myself. I would surely have wanted you to have another chance."

She searched his eyes. For some crazy reason, just knowing it hadn't been his fault made her heart lighter, even after all these years. "You didn't do it?" she asked, just to make sure.

He shook his head. "I didn't do it. I remember those days. The station was in trouble and the station manager was very edgy. People were coming and going there all the time."

She smiled at him, and a feeling of affection swept over her. "You're right. That was why you were taping that promotional spot where they wanted you to exude sex. Remember? And you got very grumpy about it."

He frowned. "I have a vague memory of doing something like that," he admitted.

She laughed softly. "I was in that spot with you. You kissed me in it."

He tried to remember, then gave it up and pulled her closer, smiling down at her, studying her pretty face. Slowly he outlined her lips with his forefinger.

"I must have amnesia," he told her softly. "Otherwise, I would surely remember."

The touch of his fingertip sent energy cascading through her bloodstream. "I'm more forgettable than you thought," she said, getting breathless.

Silver smoke seemed to fill his gaze. "Maybe I should kiss you again," he murmured. "The memory might return."

She shook her head slowly, but she couldn't pull her gaze free of his. "I don't think so."

Neither did he. Memories weren't the point now, were they? The point was the way his heart was beating, the way the blood was sizzling in his veins, the way every time he looked at her, something new inside him seemed to tighten. He had to get out of here, fast, before he did something stupid.

But he couldn't seem to move. He stood like a statue, staring down into her dark eyes. Her scent was fresh as spring and her skin was soft as April rain. He felt desire blossom in his gut like a flower from some exotic paradise, growing and spreading and filling him with a sense of intoxication. In another moment, he wouldn't be able to go at all. In another moment, he would have her.

And he couldn't do that. With effort, he wrenched himself away from her, dropping her arm and turning.

"This is goodbye, then," he said abruptly. "I'm going."

She turned and looked at him, her gaze melting in the dim light from the deck, her heart splitting in two. "Yes. You'd better go."

He started toward the door, then stopped and looked back. "Will you come over later? To see the children, I mean."

What for? Torture? So that she could see how nicely they all managed without her? "I...I don't think so. I have some things to do this afternoon. I have to work tomorrow. You know how it is."

"Come over anyway."

She turned away so that he couldn't see her face. "I don't think I should. I don't want to get too attached to the children." Oh God, how had she said that? Was it too whiny or too sarcastic? Either way, she would have been better off not saying it at all.

He turned all the way back, taking a step toward her, looking concerned. "Do you feel you're in danger of doing that?"

"Oh, yes." She half laughed, turning away. "You don't know—"

"Of course I know," he said indignantly.

She stopped where she was. "Yes, I guess you do." She hesitated for a moment, then shrugged. "Well, Marguerite is there now to take care of things."

He stiffened. "I'd better go," he said, but he still wasn't moving.

She sensed his reluctance to leave and anticipation was skittering across her nerve endings. She felt like a cat about to jump a mile high if anyone touched her—or even looked at her cross-eyed. As her gaze caught his smoldering look, something twisted deep inside. She closed her eyes, her head dropping back.

"Oh, go," she muttered. "Go quickly."

But he didn't go. Instead he erased the distance between them in one stride and took her into his arms, crushing her to him as though he'd found her in the forest or on a mountaintop, held her close, taking in her sweetness, her curves and flesh and warmth as though he could breathe it in, until he felt his insides quake.

One kiss, he told himself. That would be enough. "One kiss," he whispered to her. "Just one."

"Hurry," she whispered back, and she lifted her face, her lips parting.

He kissed he.. The room tilted and the furniture faded away and something happened to the floor. He'd never done anything quite like this before.

It started out as a kiss, plain and simple. But in seconds it morphed into a connection, a sharing, as though the beat of his pulse had joined hers, thumping faster and faster, driving him on. In the realm of his senses, the blood flowing through his body was now flowing through hers, his nerves had reached out and curled around hers, he couldn't tell where her flesh began and his ended. They were spinning, caught in a warp of chance, clinging together like two halves of one whole, holding and touching and creating something new that had never been felt or seen before.

Just one kiss, he'd said. But he'd known it was a lie when he said it.

"Jack," she gasped at last, her face still pressed to his "I forgot to breathe."

"Breathe through your nose," he muttered, nibbling on her neck. "I need your mouth."

And he found it again with his own, found the path to her heat and drank from her, while his body went to granite and his heart beat so loudly it felt as though the roar of the ocean were in his ears. He forgot he was a father, forgot his promises, his pledge. All he could remember was the fact that he was a man, and that this woman was the woman he wanted, right now, and that he mustn't hurt her.

But nothing he did at this moment could cause her pain. She was riding the gathering power of a wave she'd never dealt with before, and the thrill of it was all she knew. Her body was a miracle of sensation. She'd never known she could feel this swelling excitement, this impatience that was rapidly growing into a demand. She wanted this man, wanted him as she'd never wanted a man before. She had to have him with an urgency that felt almost wicked.

Yes, wicked, that was what it was, and being wicked was just about the most wonderful thing she'd ever done. She wanted more of it, and she slid her hands inside his open shirt to reach for it, her palms melting against muscles that rippled and contracted at her touch. He was so hard, so strong, so delicious to feel, she only wanted more of him, more to run her hands over, more to kiss her, filling her mouth with the heart and soul of him.

He was peeling away her clothes and she was glad her breasts were pretty, glad for him to see them like this, and when he touched them, kissed them, she shivered deeply and spoke in urgent whispers and prepared to take him inside her, wanted him there, had to have him with a hunger that had taken complete possession of her.

He was beautiful, his naked body a statue by Michelangelo, a poem by Donne, a sculpture by Rodin, and she knew this was right, so right, impossible to resist. It had to happen. There was no way to avoid it.

Somehow they'd made it to the bedroom and she threw herself into the tangled covers and he came down on top of her, meaning to hold back, to make sure, but she couldn't wait any longer. Crying out, she lifted to accept him and in no time at all they were both riding the wave as it crested, both driving hard and holding on tightly, clinging together as though they could never bear to be apart again. The sensation built again and again. Just when she thought it must be over, it came again, harder, higher, like a shriek in the wind, and she went for it, reaching for complete ecstasy.

And finally, there was no more. As the sweet, thrilling sensations began to fade in her, her body shuddered time and again, as though it had to find release from too much joy. At the same time, she had to turn her face away so he wouldn't see how she felt. She loved this man, loved him with all her heart, and she knew that was impossible. If only they could stay like this, holding on, two sides of the puzzle, a continuum of love and need that never ended. If only...

Jack closed his eyes, swearing silently to himself. He'd thought he had more willpower than this. And yet, as he looked at her, he knew he couldn't regret it. Leaning back, he gazed at her long, lovely body, and dreams began swirling in his head, impossible dreams, dreams of happy endings. Could it be? Was there really a chance?

He reached out one hand to touch her, to make sure she was real, that this had really happened and wasn't an illusion he'd created in his mind, but just before his hand got there, she rolled out of reach, moaning softly.

"No, this wasn't supposed to happen," she cried, hitting a pillow with her fist. "How did we let this happen?"

"I don't think we had much of a choice," he told her with a smile in his voice. "Sometimes things happen that aren't supposed to."

"You mean it was bigger than both of us?" she asked with loaded sarcasm. Groaning, she writhed in the tangled covers. "Why do we have to be so... so..."

"So damn human?" he said mildly, watching her.

"Is that what this is?" she asked, turning her head to meet his gaze. "There are plenty of people who don't give in to every stray impulse that comes along and..."

He reached out and grabbed her, pulling her naked body back to touch his. "This wasn't a stray impulse, J.J., and you know it. I don't sleep with every woman I see. I haven't touched another woman since I married my wife."

"Only me?" she asked in a small voice, searching his eyes to see if she could believe him.

He nodded. "Only you." He touched her cheek. "Didn't you like it?" he asked.

"Like it!" She let out a gust of laughter and threw her arms around his neck, arching into him and kissing him soundly on the mouth. "You took me somewhere I've never been before, Jack Remington," she whispered close to his ear. "And now, darn you, I'm going to miss it for the rest of my life."

He held her close and a feeling welled up in him. He wanted to tell her she didn't have to miss it—that he would be glad to make that special paradise a permanent refuge for the two of them to share. But she was already wriggling out of his grasp and regretting again.

"But still, this was crazy and we shouldn't have done it. I'm supposed to be concentrating on my career. You're supposed to be concentrating on your kids. We're not supposed to be here doing this." She rolled off the bed and began pulling on her clothes. "And right now I think you ought to go back to your place and be with your children. They miss you." Still only half dressed, she flew out of the room.

He knew she was right but he took his time getting ready to go. This past half hour with her had been something very special and he wanted to savor it—especially if there was very little chance that it would ever happen again.

And it couldn't happen again. She was right. They were heading in different directions and they'd paused for a moment, meeting at a crossroads. But they both had to go on with their lives. He had to concentrate on the children.

He closed his eyes for a moment, breathing deeply. There were problems he'd been avoiding while he recovered from his illness, problems that were going to have to be dealt with now that he was pretty much well again. Could he go on this way? Was it fair to his kids? Was it fair to Annie? It tore him apart to think of giving up, but he had to face facts. This illness had brought it home. That first night he was sick, he had been in no position to take care of his children, and without J.J., he hated to think of what might have happened. Did he have the right to leave his family so vulnerable to chance? Did he?

Still troubled by his thoughts, he came out into the kitchen to find J.J. sitting on a bar stool again, looking worried herself.

"We have to pretend this never happened," she told him earnestly. Her dark eyes were troubled as she gazed up into his face, and yet, there was something else there, a spark, a memory, that she couldn't hide. "We have to put this behind us and get on with our lives," she said, almost more to convince herself than to persuade him.

Despite everything, despite his agony over what to do, despite his own misgivings, her words put his back up, and when he turned to her, his mouth had a defiant set to it.

"I can't do that, J.J.," he told her. His arm shot out and curled her into his embrace, kissing her lips, her neck, her cheek, before adding softly, "and neither can you." Releasing her, he stepped back, looking her up and down as though burning her into his mind's eye. "I'll be waiting for

when you realize that," he said simply, and he turned and
left the room.

Holding her breath, she heard the front door close and
she sighed, dropping her head to the counter. He could
protest all he liked, but they had to do it. There was no other
way.

Jack got quite a welcome when he walked in the door of
his condo. Annie shrieked and launched her little body up
into his arms. Kristi echoed Annie's cry of delight and
bounced up and down on her bottom. Kathy laughed and
clapped her pudgy little hands together. Baby Mack pulled
himself up on his wobbly legs and took his first real inde-
pendent steps toward his father.

Jack grabbed him just before he tumbled and they all
laughed together. It felt damn good to be home, but when
an adult figure came into the room, he turned, half expecting J.J. for some reason, and finding instead the dour face
of Marguerite.

"Dinner be ready soon," she announced as though it
might be the coming of the grim reaper.

"Thanks for the warning," Jack murmured, but he
smiled and said louder, "Thanks for coming back so
quickly, Marguerite."

"Sure I come back. I gotta make money, don't I?" she
said gruffly, and disappeared into the kitchen.

"You got that right," he muttered, but he bent to kiss the
top of each little head before he went into the den and
picked up the telephone. Dialing long-distance, he waited
and then greeted an old friend.

"Hey, Harry? Jack Remington here. Yes, it has been a
long time. Oh, they're doing fine. Growing like weeds. Yes,
they are a handful. But listen, Harry, I've got an ulterior
motive calling you. Yes. I've got a young discovery I'd like

you to take a look at. She's very good. I'm sending you her audition tape by express mail. I'd like you to consider giving her a trial run. Yes, the morning show would do fine. No, now, I want you to look at her work first and make sure she's got what you need. The only favor I'm asking is that you take a look at her. After that, it's strictly whether she fits the bill, and I don't want you to do anything special because I'm asking. Thanks, Harry. I really appreciate it."

Putting the receiver back into its cradle, he picked up the videotape he'd been making of J.J.'s work and slipped it into an envelope. He knew what he was doing was sealing his own fate. As soon as she got a chance for New York, she'd be off like a shot. But that was what she wanted. And right now, the way he felt about her, what she wanted was what he wanted, too.

Ten

___

The babies cried half the night. J.J. lay in her bed and stared at the ceiling and cried along with them. She longed to hold Kathy and tickle Baby Mack and push Kristi in her little swing. She wondered if someone had made sure Annie got to bed on time. After all, she had school in the morning. And when she finally dragged herself up just before dawn, she had to exert all her willpower to keep from calling and offering the little girl a ride.

Her eyes were red and her face was drawn, but she worked some magic with makeup and went on in to work. Luckily she had only a few minutes of on-camera duty that morning, and she could stay in the background for the most part. At one point she took some papers into the copy center to be reproduced, and found Bob Newton, the feisty station manager, finishing up some copying of his own.

"Hi," she said, remembering the doughnut incident.

"Hi," he returned rather gruffly, possibly remembering it, too.

She hesitated, knowing this was the man Jack said he'd once worked with. She desperately needed to know more about what Jack had been doing over the past ten years. This was probably her one and only chance to find anything out. Giving the man a wide smile, she approached.

"You know, I've been meaning to ask you something. I hear you once worked with Jack Remington."

He turned his grizzled head and frowned at her. "Who told you that?"

She smiled, not answering his question. "Tell me about him," she said instead, plopping her own papers down on the machine. "I used to work with him once myself, but I lost touch with him over the years. How's he been?"

He stared at her for a long moment, then seemed to decide she might not be as much a waste of time as he had once thought. Leaning against the copy machine, he folded his arms across his chest and looked thoughtful.

"Well, let's see. You can start off with the fact that he was a damn good anchorman. One of the best. He had talent and intelligence. You don't often get both in one man."

She smiled. She liked hearing that. "Yes, he was good, wasn't he?"

He looked at her sharply, as though curious about her angle. "Of course, he'll never work again," he said flatly.

She gasped. "What . . . why do you say that?"

"Ah, he was ruined." He waved a hand as though dismissing the thought. "It was that wife of his. What was her name? She's the one who ruined him."

"Ruined him?" This was the first she'd heard about this and it chilled her. She moved a little closer and stared at him intensely. "What do you mean?"

"She was beautiful, a high-fashion model. She was in all the magazines and in the society press. It was when we were working together in San Francisco. He went nuts over her and then made the mistake of marrying her."

"I . . . I suppose he loved her."

"Naw. He only thought he did. They had nothing in common. He was dazzled by that glitzy stuff, but he learned his lesson. She was hell on wheels, demanding they live the jet-set life, when all he wanted to do was work."

J.J. nodded numbly. "What happened to her?"

"Last I heard, she died in childbirth or something. Happened about a year ago."

That would fit with things Annie had said. She ached for those innocent children. "What a tragedy."

"Yeah?" He shrugged. "You might say that, if she hadn't brought it on herself."

J.J. frowned, unable to connect that comment with anything she knew about. "What do you mean by that?"

But Bob seemed to have had enough of this. He straightened and frowned at her fiercely. "What do you mean by asking me all these questions? What business is it of yours?"

"I...uh..." She tried to think of a good excuse and failed.

"Yes, I know he's living in that condo right next to the one we put you in." He shook his head, looking disgusted with it all, but rather pleased that he'd startled her. "Big mistake. Every woman who lives in that place falls in love with the guy. But he's committed to his kids and he tells each and every one of them to take a hike."

She blinked and tried to smile. "Does he?"

"Hasn't he told you yet? He will." He chuckled, seeming to find that very funny. "Oh yes, he will." His gaze sharpened. "In the meantime, get back to work. There's too much gossiping that goes on around here. Women. They just can't stop talking." And he was gone in a flutter of papers and a slamming of the door.

J.J. took a deep breath. "Whew," she muttered to herself. But at least she'd found out some things she hadn't known before, and had some new questions, as well. Had Jack been unhappily married? Too bad she couldn't ask him.

She thought about Jack all day and when she went home, she listened but there was no sound from next door. She picked up the invitation to the shower that Jack had left sitting on her counter and looked at it. Moving like a woman in a trance, she dialed the number of her agent in California.

"Mike, can you get me out of working next weekend?" she asked.

"Isn't that the prime-time anchor spot they've given you?"

"Yes, but..."

"Are you crazy?" His voice went higher than she would have thought possible.

"Listen," she said quickly, "my old college roommate who I haven't seen for ten years is having a baby shower and all my roommates will be there and it's the first time in—"

"Listen yourself, sugar baby," he responded acidly. "I told you this was your last chance, didn't I? And you want to go and throw it all away for a baby shower?"

"But Mike, it's her first baby. In fact, it's the first for anyone from our group. It's in Denver and I won't have time to go and come back—"

"Here's a hot tip, doll. If you do go, don't come back." He laughed at his own joke. "Don't be nuts, honey. I've talked to the people there at the station and they like you. Don't rock the boat. Just remember, New York is more likely to be watching this than anything else you've done. If you're not there, they won't see you."

She sighed, feeling defeated. "I guess you're right," she said in a small voice. "Okay. Goodbye, Mike."

She sat very still and thought very hard. Things weren't going well at the moment. Too many things seemed off kilter and she couldn't stand it. She had to know how the triplets were. She had to make sure Annie was being allowed to be a little girl at least part of the day. And she had to see Jack again.

He said he'd be waiting for her. She rose, her heart in her throat. What if she just went over? Just for a minute. Just to see.

She got as far as the door before she stopped herself. If she went over, she might never be able to come back. With a moan, she spun and flung herself onto the couch. Once, the only thing she'd really wanted was fame and fortune. Now things seemed so much more complicated. She put her head in her hands. If only she could think things through clearly. If only... If only...

The next day when she opened her mailbox and drew out her mail, the stack included a large piece of paper folded small. It opened like an origami puzzle and when she finally spread it wide on her counter, it turned out to be a painting by A. Remigon, which seemed to be as much as Annie could handle of her name.

A painting. Her breath caught in her throat. Annie had given her a painting. She traced the outline of the picture with her finger. It was a little girl with golden hair and very big eyes. A self-portrait? She remembered what Annie had once told her—that she was saving all her paintings for her new mother.

"Oh, Annie," she whispered, tears welling in her eyes. "I only wish it were true."

* * *

Jack came in from a trip to the park with a baby on each arm and Annie pushing the stroller with Baby Mack bouncing and laughing in the front seat.

"We're home," he called out.

"We're home," Annie echoed, looking up at his face and laughing at him. They both knew Marguerite was not about to call back.

He smiled down at his little love and his heart seemed to crack open in his chest. That feeling of desperation caught at him again. What was he going to do? How was he going to save his family? He swung his two charges into a bear hug and noticed they needed changing.

"Come on, you two," he muttered. "Annie, could you let Baby Mack out to crawl around for a few minutes?"

Annie did as she was told, struggling a little, but practice had made her pretty good at these tasks. In no time, the boy was scuttling across the floor, and pulling himself up at the edge of the couch and trying out his walking form, only to land with a plunk on his bottom.

"Dinner gonna be ready soon," Marguerite said from the doorway to the kitchen, her face surly.

Annie danced toward her. "Marguerite, can I help you make dinner?" she cried hopefully, her curls bouncing.

The woman's frown darkened and her mouth turned down at the corners. "No. You just get in my way."

Annie stopped short, her eyes wide. "J.J. let me help," she noted softly, as though she thought that might persuade the woman.

But Marguerite wasn't going to use J.J. as a role model. She sniffed, her nose in the air. "That girl don't know what she's doing," she said shortly. "She *needs* help, she does." And she turned back to the kitchen.

Jack, coming into the room with a newly cleaned Kristi, caught the end of that. "Never mind, Annie," he said, ruffling her hair. "You can help me set the table."

"Okay," she said, but obviously that wasn't quite as exciting as learning to cook would be.

He watched her as she pondered over the silverware, carefully picking which pieces to use, her lower lip caught in her teeth as she concentrated, and his mind went back to thoughts he'd been having for the past few days. Something had to change. He couldn't put this child through this forever.

"This one?" she asked, holding up a gnarled-looking fork he'd inherited from his grandmother.

He nodded. "Give that one to me," he told her. "That one is perfect."

Watching as she carefully carried it to the table, he ached for her. Poor Annie. She was the one who had really ended up with the short end of the stick in the situation. Here she was dealing with a grumpy housekeeper and an absent-minded father and three little babies not much younger than she was. She had to be daughter, sister and little mother all in one.

It was too much to ask of any child. And yet, what were his options? Life wasn't fair. Never had been, never would be. You took whatever life had to throw at you and either you ducked out of the way or you reached out and caught hold of it. The only other choice was taking it square in the face. And he had the scars to prove it.

He watched his daughter laying out the silverware on the table and he swore obscenely to himself. Tough talk was great, but where did it leave Annie? It was time to face facts. Things had to change.

The doorbell rang and his heart stopped, then started to beat again as though he'd been running hard. His heart had been doing this for the past two days, every time the phone rang, every time there was someone at the door. Annie ran to answer the bell and he held his breath.

"J.J.!" he heard her exclaim. "I'm helping Daddy set the table."

Jack closed his eyes for a moment, sagging against the wall and half laughing. She'd come. Thank God. She'd finally come.

By the time she entered the room, he was looking cool and confident again, and he grinned at her jauntily.

"You're just in time for dinner," he told her, his blue eyes sparkling.

Her cheeks were flushed and her eyes were full of doubts. She looked at him and thought she'd never seen a man look better. The afternoon sunlight was glinting on his tan face and his dark hair was slightly mussed and falling over his forehead. He looked graceful and sexy and infinitely huggable. But she couldn't think about that, could she?

"I . . . I had to come and see how the children were doing," she claimed lamely.

"We're all doing just fine," he told her, his blue-eyed gaze capturing hers. "Even me."

"I'm glad," she said faintly. "I . . ."

"You'll stay for dinner," he insisted.

"Oh, but I can't—"

"Yes, you can. Marguerite, we've got another one for dinner," he called into the kitchen.

J.J. felt as though she were moving in some sort of slow motion. She couldn't think of the right things to say. Dropping to sit on the couch, she mostly smiled and let the babies crawl all over her and listened to Annie happily recite everything that had happened to her for the past forty-eight hours.

But her gaze kept straying to fasten on Jack, and every time it did, her breath seemed to come a little more quickly.

The children were a joy. They gurgled and cooed and snuggled into her arms and generally made her feel that they'd missed her. When Marguerite announced dinner, she helped strap the babies into high chairs and found she was actually staying to eat with them, whether she liked it or not.

"What's for dinner?" Jack asked Marguerite as he followed her into the kitchen to help serve it.

"Pot roast," she announced shortly, pausing a moment to glare at J.J. "Is my very good pot roast."

J.J.'s gaze met Annie's and she saw the panic in her eyes. Reaching out, J.J. took her hand and pulled her close. "Sit next to me," she whispered to her. "Don't worry. We'll handle this."

Annie's face fell even further when she saw the pile of lima beans on her plate. The mashed potatoes were her only solace, and she ate those quickly. J.J. cut up the hunk of pot roast for her, dividing the lean meat from the fat, but the poor girl still couldn't face it.

J.J. hesitated. The most straightforward thing would be to say something to Jack, or to confront Marguerite directly. But Jack already looked like a juggler with too many plates in the air, and the last time Marguerite had heard criticism about her pot roast, she'd stormed off and quit. This time, subterfuge would have to suffice.

The babies were banging their hands on the trays of their high chairs and making a ruckus, and J.J. used the commotion to hide the fact that she was sneaking bites from Annie's plate and eating them herself whenever Marguerite wasn't looking. But she had to eat her own portion, as well, and pretty soon she'd reached her capacity for tough meat and tasteless beans.

One more bite is all I can handle, she told herself, spearing a particularly stringy piece of meat and shuddering as she popped it into her own mouth. She chewed hard, popping the bite from one side to the other, and then, in mid-chew, she lifted her gaze and found Jack staring at her from across the table with a puzzled frown on his face. There was no telling how long he'd been watching.

Well, actually, there was. It was obvious he'd seen the whole thing and couldn't imagine what sort of woman would be taking meat from Annie when she wasn't looking. J.J. flushed and tried to smile, but she knew she looked as guilty as though she'd been stealing food out of a baby's mouth.

"Would you like me to get you some more from the kitchen?" he asked her.

She shook her head and colored all the more. Did he really think she was eating Annie's meat because she was hungry? The humiliation was staggering, but she didn't know how she could explain to him right now.

The main problem was, how were they going to get rid of the rest of the food on Annie's plate? The little girl had downed her milk and polished off her mashed potatoes and a roll, along with a healthy serving of salad. She wasn't going to starve, at any rate. But there was still an ugly hunk of gristly meat on her plate, and that pile of lima beans. Turning, she looked up at J.J. expectantly.

"Marguerite will be mad," she whispered, reminding her. Her dark eyes were huge and worried.

J.J. nodded, but she knew there was no way any more food could be shoveled in. There was only one other solution, and luckily, the napkins were paper. And at that moment, Kathy showed off major league potential as she pitched a handful of mashed potatoes against the wall, drawing Jack's attention and making Marguerite head for the kitchen for a washcloth, muttering dire threats.

"Here," J.J. whispered to Annie, passing her the napkin. "Wrap it up and hand it back to me. I'll take care of it."

Annie did a quick and creditable job of it, though she did squash a few lima beans between her fingers and had to be cleaned up. Now J.J. was sitting with a wad of food twisted into a napkin in her lap. Marguerite came out of the kitchen with the washcloth. J.J. smiled at her innocently. The woman glared daggers back, but proceeded to the wall to wipe up the potato remnants. J.J. took advantage of the moment to rise and slip into the kitchen to find the trash container.

She glanced around and opened a couple of cupboards, but she couldn't find anything that would fit the bill. Then she noticed a brown paper bag standing alone in the corner. Peeking inside, she saw what looked like discarded papers. Relieved, she tossed in the heavy napkin and turned just in time to face Marguerite's suspicious look as she stomped into the kitchen.

"What that you do?" Marguerite demanded, her pale green eyes glittering. "That not trash, you know."

J.J. gasped and turned back toward the bag, but Marguerite beat her to it, yanking out the napkin, which immediately spilled its contents all over the floor.

"Good food!" Marguerite shouted. "Look, mister. Come here fast. She throw away my good food!"

Bright red, J.J. could hardly manage to gargle out a confused explanation, as Jack and Annie, drawn by the shouts, gaped at the two of them from the doorway.

"Marguerite, calm down," Jack ordered, trying to take charge of a situation he didn't yet understand. "I'm sure she didn't mean to insult you in any way."

"Of course not," J.J. insisted brightly. "You're a very good cook, Marguerite. The meat was quite tasty. Only..." She searched her brain wildly for a story that might fly. "Only I have a dietary problem I was too embarrassed to tell you about, and—"

"She throw away good food," Marguerite cried triumphantly. She jerked her thumb like a baseball umpire. "She goes."

Jack stared at her incredulously. "I hardly think that follows as a matter of course," he said dryly.

Marguerite was putting her foot down and she shook her head adamantly. "I can't stay here if you gonna keep this bad woman," she said, confident in her power.

Jack's expression hardened as Annie gasped and J.J. rolled her eyes.

"Marguerite," he said through gritted teeth. "This bad woman, as you call her, is worth ten of you. She stays."

Marguerite sniffed. "Then I go."

Jack's eyes were cold as flint, his jaw like a rock. "That's fine with me." He pulled out his wallet and extracted a few large bills. "This ought to cover what you're owed, plus a couple of weeks' salary. It's been interesting knowing you."

J.J. gasped, looking from one to the other of them. Marguerite took the money and began to pack up her things, her lips set tightly. Slinging her prized paper bag up into her arms, she left the room, and J.J. pulled Jack aside, whispering to him urgently.

"Jack! You can't do this. You can't get rid of her, not for me. I won't be here much longer. You know I can't stay."

He looked down at her and couldn't resist touching her cheek gently with one finger. "I know you can't." Looking around, he realized they were the only ones left in the kitchen, and beyond all reason, pulled her close, kissing her quickly before releasing her and returning to a decorous distance apart.

"But J.J.," he told her earnestly, looking deeply into her dark eyes, "just watching you with the children has made me realize what a mistake it is to cling to Marguerite just because she's willing to do work I need done. My children need someone who loves them, not someone who just keeps them clean. Look at the way Annie invests love in Marguerite and look at how little the woman gives back to her."

J.J. knew that he was right. She'd been struck by the same disparity. Annie deserved better, and so did Jack and the babies. Marguerite should go.

She almost laughed aloud, thinking of how jealous she'd been of the woman before she'd met her, then sobered as the front door slammed. Marguerite was gone. Jack and the children were alone.

"What are you going to do?" she asked him.

He shrugged. "Hire someone for the few days we have left, then head for Denver." He turned back toward where the triplets were beginning to get fussy, still strapped in their high chairs with only Annie to watch them. "You sure you couldn't get off and come with us?" he asked, only half seriously.

"I wish I could," she said, following him out to the dining room.

He turned back and stared at her, struck by the depth of feeling in her voice, but she gave him a jaunty smile and walked right past, taking Baby Mack up into her arms and cooing to him as she began to clean up his grubby little face.

A terrible resolve was growing in her. It had been awfully brave of Jack to get rid of Marguerite that way, with no backup in the wings. If Jack could be brave, so could she. Yes, so could she.

Eleven

———

J.J. went right into Bob Newton's sumptuously furnished office without waiting for the receptionist to announce her. Her feet sank into the plush carpet, making her feel as though she needed snowshoes to get across it, but that didn't slow her down a bit.

"Mr. Newton, I have a very big favor to ask you. Could I please have next weekend off?"

He frowned at her, taking off his glasses to get a better look.

"No," he said shortly.

She leaned on the desk with both hands and looked earnestly into his eyes, her jet black hair loose and swinging about her shoulders. "I really need it off. There is something I must do."

"I'm giving you a shot at the anchor position on the weekend." He pulled his head back as though resisting all that earnestness. "What's the matter with you? You can't put that off until some other time. It's now or never."

"I know that. I...I'll have to give it up. I need that weekend. It's so important. There's no way I can work."

He shrugged, his eyes hard and impassive, the ultimate implacable boss. "Then you'll have to quit," he told her bluntly. "I won't change the work schedule."

She took a deep breath and closed her eyes for a moment, then smiled at him.

"Okay. I quit." She half gasped as she said the words, hardly believing she could do it. But as the realization began to sink in, she felt a bubble of happiness start in her chest.

But there was no happiness across the desk. Bob stared at her, slowly shaking his head.

"It's that damn Jack Remington, isn't it?" he muttered, glowering. "Admit it. It's him."

She lifted her chin and smiled at him again. "Yes. I have to help him take his children to Denver."

"You're a fool," he barked.

She laughed. "I know." She wanted to dance the way Annie did when she was happy. "Isn't it wonderful?"

He glared, as though he thought the force of his will might make her change her mind. "Clear your desk out and don't come back."

"Okay." Impulsively she leaned across the desk and kissed the man right on the top of his balding head. "Thank you, Mr. Newton. And wish me luck."

"I wish you'd get a brain in your head," he muttered as she whirled out of his office. "And I wish I could bottle what that guy's got. I'd be a millionaire."

* * *

She dreaded the call she was going to have to make to Mike, her agent, but when she got home, her answering machine was blinking, and she found he'd already heard.

"Are you nuts? Are you out of your mind? Have you gone loco? Are you smoking something? You don't quit a job like that. You're crazy, and if you don't go back and eat humble pie to get your place back, I'm going to have to drop you as a client. You hear that? Drop you cold."

J.J. heard his words, sentiments that would once have chilled her to the bone, and she found herself smiling. Good old Mike. He would never change. But she had.

"Go ahead and drop me, Mike," she murmured as he went on with the threats. "I've got other things on my mind right now." She shook her head and talked as though he could hear her. "Did you know there are other things in life, Mike? Did you know that people are out there living real lives while we are all caught up in who is going to anchor what show? Did you know that it doesn't really matter to most of the universe?"

The sound of Mike's other line ringing could be heard in the background, stopping his diatribe for the moment.

"I've got a call from New York coming in. I'll call you back."

His voice clicked out, then came back again.

"Hi, it's me." His voice had changed. The anger was gone. And so were the threats to drop her. "Say, listen, doll, I just got the strangest call from New York. Who do you know, darling? What's going on?" He named the network. "They want you for their morning show the fourteenth of next month. For one whole week." He sounded as though he'd been running hard, his breath coming in gulps. "J.J., do you know what this means? What can I say? This is it, J.J. This is it. Call me when you get in. I don't know what to say, except, hey, you're obviously doing something right and anyway, hey, I'm a great agent, aren't I? Call me. Call me right now!''

J.J. sat where she was, stunned. New York. It had finally happened. Her big break was being handed to her. They wanted her in New York on the fourteenth to work the morning show. It was a dream come true. The only question was, did she still care? And the answer to that one wasn't easy.

Later, Jack stopped by and she told him about her extraordinary day, and she found herself telling him about quitting, but not about New York.

"You quit?" He stared at her. "Are you sure you want to do that?"

She nodded happily, her eyes shining. "Oh, yes. I have no doubts at all."

How could she doubt? As far as she was concerned, she was getting the best of all possible worlds—having her cake and eating it, too. She was going to go to Denver with Jack and his kids, she was going to see all her old friends at Sara's baby shower, and she was going to fly off to New York to get her shot at the big time. What more could she ask for?

She got busy playing games with the babies, and Jack watched her, frowning, but he didn't say any more at the time. His feelings were mixed and he hated that. He liked it when the way ahead looked straight and rutless, with no side streets and forks in the road. He didn't want to have to think things over, worry them, make decisions that caused pain. But this was one of those times when such things seemed to be unavoidable.

He hesitated, still troubled by her actions. "Giving up a job is a profound thing to do. It will make a lot of changes in your life."

She smiled at him sweetly. "It's not nearly as profound as getting fired," she said. "And I've lived through that."

He frowned. "You're not going to accuse me of that again, are you?"

She shook her head. "No. But I did survive. And I will again."

"What did Bob say when you told him you were quitting?" he asked.

She laughed comfortably, looking at him with an open affection that startled him. "He said, 'It's that damn Jack Remington, isn't it?'"

Jack's brows drew together. "What made him think this had anything to do with me?" he asked her.

She raised one eyebrow. "He thinks all the women who live in this condo end up...uh...falling for you." At the last moment, she stumbled over the words, not wanting to reveal herself fully. "He seems very jealous to me."

He groaned, throwing his head back. "You told him the truth, didn't you?"

She took a sip of coffee and carefully set the mug back down on the coffee table. "I don't know, Jack," she said, looking at him with clear eyes. "What is the truth?"

He shrugged as though it were self-evident. "That you want to go to your friend's baby shower."

Her eyes darkened and she regarded him with her head to the side. "Ah, is that it?"

He frowned at the tone of her voice. "Don't you?"

She smiled at him. "Of course."

"That's what I thought," he said, relieved.

"It has nothing at all to do with you."

"Of course not."

"Bob Newton doesn't know what he's talking about," she said, throwing out a hand as though to dismiss the very idea. "Why, you're hardly even attractive. I mean, you're an awfully nice guy, but as far as sweeping women off their feet—he just doesn't understand about that."

"No," he said, looking at her with a veiled gaze. "Surely not."

She smiled. "You do have these gorgeous muscles," she noted, eyeing his most visible biceps, "and shoulders you could build a fort on."

"J.J.!" he exclaimed, half laughing, half embarrassed.

She bit back an impish grin. "And blue eyes that seem to capture the light of the stars at times," she continued, stretching toward him like a cat wanting to be stroked. "And a fair-to-middling profile . . ."

The scent of her hair, the glow in her eyes, the sense of her warm body so close, all combined to overcome his good intentions. Desire burst inside him as though it had been waiting to explode, and his instincts were to grab her, to take her in a quick and sudden conquest, satisfy his need. But quick on the heels of his animal reaction came his intellect and even more importantly, his emotions. He cared for her, cared probably more than he should.

He kissed her. He kissed her long and hard and hot and then he drew back, groaning, and tried to put a stop to it.

"J.J., I didn't come over to do this," he murmured, his eyes tortured.

She reached up and touched his lips. "You should have," she whispered, her melting gaze connecting with his. "It needs to be done."

Whether it needed to be done or not, it was going to happen. His hands slid beneath her sweater and cupped her breasts and she writhed in his grasp, her senses reacting to the thought of what he was about to do as much as to what he was doing. She reached for his crisp white shirt, unbuttoning the top button, and then her long fingers snapped open button after button with ease, working more and more quickly as his hands found her most vulnerable places and caressed and molded until she was twisting out of her sweater, needing to feel her breasts pressing against his hard, silky skin.

The couch made a perfect love nest. There were arms to brace against and pillows to shove out of the way. There was a structure for positions that made them laugh and other positions that made sweet sense. They explored and tested and made new magic, and all the while, each was holding back the need to make this game play out its natural course.

His body was so beautiful in the lamplight, like liquid gold, and it responded to her hand in ways that made her tremble with excitement. This was hers, at least for the moment.

His touch was slow and easy, stroking and gliding, testing and teasing, until she cried out with frustration and pulled him to her with a growl that came from deep inside her. He joined with her and very quickly took her back to paradise, a place she'd only been to once before, and only with him, only in his arms.

Higher and higher, like birds soaring through clouds, until they reached a place where there was only sunshine, rich and clean and blinding, so intense, it felt as though the sun itself were bursting inside her. And as they floated gently back down to earth, she felt tears spilling down her cheeks, and she laughed with delight, because they were hot tears of pure joy.

I love you. She wanted to say it aloud, but she didn't dare. So she said it with her body, with her hands, with the look in her eyes. And she wondered if he heard her.

His hand stroked down the length of her body and he marveled at how satisfied he felt. He'd had women before, in his younger days, lots of them. And he'd enjoyed lovemaking. But there had always been a sense of expectations unfulfilled in the past—as though his soul had not quite found what it was looking for. There was none of that now, and there hadn't been the other day, either. Somehow, with J.J., there was a sense of completion, as though it were so right, so fine, nothing could ever be better. This was all there was, and it was exactly right. With this woman, he could be content.

She rolled over and looked at him, feeling his satisfaction and sharing it. But there were things she still needed from him, things only he could give her, chances she had to take.

"Tell me about your wife," she said, and then held her breath, wondering if she had gone too far. Was this the worst time to ask that? Or the best?

He was still for a moment, then he turned and looked at the window. "Her name was Phoebe," he said. "She was very beautiful."

"Yes." She took a deep breath, relieved. At least he wasn't angry she'd asked. "I've seen her picture." He didn't volunteer anything else, so finally she asked in a very small voice, "Did you love her very much?"

"No," he responded, making her gasp. "Not really. Oh, I thought I did when I first married her. But I knew in a month that I'd made a mistake."

"Oh," she said weakly. "I . . . I didn't realize—"

"No, of course not. How could you know? I've never told anyone else. Except Phoebe." He turned and looked at her, his blue eyes black in the lamplight. "But the children must never know."

"Of course not. Oh, no, of course not," she added, realizing what he meant, realizing what trust he was putting in her and loving him for it.

"I wanted to call it quits as soon as I knew we weren't right for each other. But by then, Annie was on the way."

"Oh. Oh, Jack, that's too bad."

"I thought I could stick it out for Annie's sake, but things got worse and worse." He turned and stared at her, hard. "I'm telling you all this now," he warned her. "But I'll never talk about it again."

She nodded, not saying a word, tingling with a sense of the faith he had, praying she would be worthy of it.

He stared at her for a long moment, then seemed to be comfortable with her response and went on.

"We really weren't good for each other. Neither one of us was happy. But she was afraid to go it alone. It got so bad, I told her I wanted to go and take Annie with me. She got hysterical and..." He turned away. "Well, I won't go into the gory details. What happened was, she got pregnant again to force me to stay."

J.J. swallowed hard and looked away, as well, not knowing what she could say or do to ease his pain. Just listen, she supposed. Not that she could think of anything else. The agony Jack must have endured—and the agony his poor wife had gone through—was more than she'd expected. People shouldn't have to be so miserable or live such confused lives.

"The triplets were born, and she died with complications. She saw them that first day, and then she slipped away."

"Oh, Jack." She put a hand on his arm and he stared down at it as though he weren't sure what it was.

"The hell of it is, my children lost their mother. They'll have a hard time getting over that. But the miracle is, I've got all four of them." He raised his head and looked directly into her eyes. "And believe me, J.J., I would go through it all again just to have that."

She understood. Of course he would. And so would she, darn it. Those children...

The warning Mrs. Lark had given her flashed in her mind.
"It's too late, Mrs. Lark," she whispered.

Jack didn't understand her words, but felt her empathy,
and he gathered her in his arms and hid his face in her hair.
"That's it," he muttered abruptly. "Want to make love?"

She chuckled low in her throat. "Isn't that what we just
did?"

He hugged her closer, looking at her pink-tipped breasts,
feeling his body respond with a new arousal. "If you think
we're going to stop with one time, you'd better make some
adjustments in your expectations."

She laughed and lay back in his arms. "Okay, Casa-
nova," she told him. "I'm adjusted. Let's see what you can
do."

He showed her that, surprising her with his tender touch,
and she was gasping for breath when it was over.

"J. J. Jensen," he told her, stroking her hair. "You're a
lovely, passionate woman. Why aren't you married to some
nice guy and living in the suburbs?"

She stiffened, reacting automatically to the veiled criticism just as she always did. And then she relaxed. He wasn't
chiding her the way others always did. He was just curious.

"I think it's hard to jump into marriage when the only
one you've seen up close and personal was a bad one," she
said hesitantly. Turning, she looked into space to avoid his
eyes. "When you're young, you see these families on television or in the movies, and they seem so happy, so full of
love and caring for one another. And when you don't have
that in your own family, your heart yearns so hard . . ." Her
voice caught and she tried to turn it into a laugh and failed.

His hand covered hers. "I'm sorry," he said simply.

She glanced at him and tried to smile. "It wasn't your
fault."

"No. But no one asks for the family they end up with. It's all the luck of the draw. And I guess you had a bad hand."

She nodded and went on softly, telling him about her father's disappearance and her mother's inattention. "I sound like I'm whining," she said impatiently. "I...I guess I love them. They're my family. But they didn't raise me in any way that made me want to replicate that experience in my own life."

"There are other families. Good ones."

"I know. I just never had the nerve to play that game of chance again."

He smiled at her, but his smile turned into a frown as he caught sight of the clock behind her. Time was slipping away and he'd left his children too long. Mrs. Lark probably needed to get home soon. He began dressing quickly.

"Now, what was it I came over here for?" he muttered as he searched for his shoes.

"To make sure I'd done the right thing by quitting at the station," she reminded him, smiling indulgently as she slipped back into her own clothes.

"Oh. Right." He looked at her sharply. "And you're sure?"

She nodded, and he hesitated.

"Does this mean you've given up on a career in TV?" he asked, searching her face.

"Oh no," she said quickly, shaking her head.

He nodded as though that pleased him. "Good. Because...well, you never know. There just might be other opportunities about to knock on your door. Keep your hopes up."

His words took a few minutes to sink in. As she saw him to the door and kissed him a quick goodbye, their meaning percolated, and as the door shut, the implications came through quite clearly.

Jack was the one who had finagled the place on the morning show in New York. Of course. Why hadn't she realized it from the first? What sort of fool was she? Why would this land in her lap out of the blue, after all these years? Jack did it. He really did have connections in the big time, and he did it for her.

And she'd known it, deep inside—which was why she had hesitated in mentioning it to him. Of course.

She sank to sit on a bar stool and stare into the darkened kitchen. She didn't know whether to laugh or cry.

"Oh, Jack," she murmured with a sigh. "Oh, you darling jerk."

The next few days flew by as they prepared for the journey to Denver. Jack had a van and they spent time fixing it up as a rolling nursery. J.J. took care of the babies while Jack did the work that needed to be done on the vehicle, then he traded off and watched them while she went grocery shopping and packed clothes and baby accoutrements.

The babies were getting to be more of a handful every day. They were into everything and moving so quickly it was hard to keep track of them. The little girls were quick learners. Once they saw Baby Mack up and walking, it was as though they looked at each other and said, "Hey! That's cool!" And they were up and running in no time at all.

"No more little babies," J.J. said nostalgically. "They're toddlers now."

The words were hardly out of her mouth before a crash came from the bedroom and she raced in to find that Kristi had pulled the changing table over on herself. Luckily she wasn't hurt. But it was only one incident in a day that was filled with them.

A huge storm blew through a day or so before they were due to leave, and that turned out to be a blessing in disguise, because it gave them a day to rest before the trip.

They spent time playing games with the children and playing song tapes and singing along. When an unusual snow flurry hit town, they dressed everyone warmly and went out into it for a few minutes, just to share in the miracle. And finally the babies went to sleep and Annie found a television program she liked, and Jack and J.J. had a short time for peaceful coexistence, side by side on the couch in the living room of Jack's condo.

They talked and teased and laughed—and then J.J. brought up a subject that had been bothering her for some time. She knew how devoted Jack was to his children, how hard he'd worked to keep the family together. And she'd noticed some new currents in the air lately. She wanted to get to the bottom of things.

"Jack," she probed tentatively. "Why...why exactly are you going to Denver?"

He knew right away what she was getting at, and his face tightened. "I'm taking the children to see their grandparents."

She nodded slowly. "And then what?" she asked him, her voice soft.

"And then..." His voice started out the sentence with the same hearty tone he'd used before, but he saw the look on her face and he gave up the pretense. For eleven months he'd been adamantly, fiercely opposed to the plan he was facing. But he'd begun to realize that his most fundamental principles were wavering. He hated it. But it was true. For some time now, he'd begun to doubt he really could do this thing. Some days it was just too damn hard.

"I don't know, J.J.," he said quietly. "I haven't decided."

Her eyes looked like smudges of soot on her face. "You're going to leave them there, aren't you?"

He turned slowly toward her, his own eyes tortured. "I don't know what else I can do, J.J. That night when I got sick was a wake-up call. I couldn't handle it. My babies were unprotected here. If you hadn't come along when you did, I don't know what might have happened." He shrugged, feeling helpless, feeling ill. "I can't risk hurting them," he said, his voice shaking. "I just can't do that."

She touched his cheek and brushed back his hair, wishing she could say or do something to take away the pain and give him back his babies. But she couldn't. She didn't have the right to promise anything.

Still it broke her heart to see him like this, killed her to think of those children without him. Something had to be done . . . somehow. If only she could think of what.

Twelve

Two days later, J.J. was on the road. It was exciting taking off down the highway with the Remington family—including the cat—and feeling like part of it. The babies were charming and playful or frowning and fussy, or asleep, and seldom at the same time. Annie was a big help most of the time, but she did tend to drive adults crazy with the age-old question "Are we there yet?" every five minutes from the moment they left home.

The rhythm of the car was therapeutic for the babies. As the trip wore on and the excitement faded, they did a lot of sleeping, and that gave J.J. time to sit up front with Jack and think. She hadn't had much time to do that in the past few days, and there were things that needed mulling over.

The week had been hectic. She'd had to move out of the condo right away. It belonged to the station, and once she no longer worked for them, she had to get out. Luckily there wasn't much to pack, and what she did have she'd moved

next door to Jack's, and then right into the van for the trip
to Denver. From then on the focus had been on preparing
the condo to be left and the children to be taken. Now that
she had a moment to breathe, she sat back and realized this
might be the last twenty-four hours she ever spent with Jack.
The thought was not a pleasant one.

They'd started the trip late at night and were driving
straight through to Denver. It would have been nice to have
started in daylight and stopped at a motel halfway there to
rest, but not many places would have accepted a crew like
theirs very easily, so it seemed best to push on and make it
in one pass. The road conditions were still a bit dicey in
some areas, especially at the higher elevations, and they
swept down highways where snow was piled high along the
sides, turning the landscape into an eerie icy tunnel that enchanted J.J., the California girl.

"Now this is what I call winter," she noted, staring out at
what the headlights revealed.

"Enjoy it while you can. Spring should be here about next
week," Jack told her.

Next week. She should be in New York by then. She ought
to tell him. But then, he probably knew, didn't he? She
glanced at him and decided it was time to get it out in the
open.

"I've had an offer from New York," she said quietly,
watching his reaction. "They want me to do the morning
show for a week. I start the fourteenth."

"No kidding?" He glanced at her out of the corner of his
eye. "That's great," he said a little too heartily. "Wow, I'm
really happy for you. That's great."

She bit back a smile. It was a good thing he'd never gone
into acting. "Yes, it's what I've always dreamed of, my big
chance." *And I owe it all to you,* she could have added. But
he obviously didn't want her to know.

He nodded, though his hands seemed to be clenching the wheel. "Are you excited about it?" he asked.

"Oh, yes. Definitely."

He nodded again, though he didn't look very happy. "You'll do well in New York. You've got what it takes. Just remember one thing." He glanced at her again. "Don't let them make you into something that you're not. Keep what makes you unique. Don't become one of the plastic people."

She raised a hand as though swearing in. "Cross my heart and hope to die," she told him. "I won't do that."

"Good. Stick to that pledge and you'll make a name for yourself." He grinned, suddenly looking much happier. "Speaking of names, now that we're alone, it's time you told me the truth."

"What truth?" she asked airily, pretending not to know what he was driving at. "Don't tell me you want to know if I dye my hair?"

"No, not that. I want to know what J.J. stands for."

She turned away abruptly. "No. No one needs to know that," she said firmly.

"Okay, don't tell me both at once. Just the first one. Tell me that."

She hesitated. There was no real reason not to reveal it, but she enjoyed stringing him along, and anyway, it was just such a silly name, one of the many things she held against her parents to this day.

"I'm not going to tell you," she said. "But I'll give you a hint. Think about the crazy mood society was going through around the time I was born, and know that my father's best friend named his son who was born in the same month Happy Apple." She shuddered just thinking of it. "I was told they were all attending a love-in at the time the name choice was made."

"Oh, my God," Jack said, looking sincerely disturbed as he pulled the van onto a new highway and looked over at her. "Maybe you're right. Maybe I don't really want to know."

She nodded, her lips tight. "As far as I'm concerned, my official name is J.J. Let's leave it at that."

"If you insist." He grinned at her. "Just promise me it's not Jumping Jellybeans."

She laughed. "I promise. Now leave it alone."

Baby Mack was stirring and she released her seat belt and went back to care for him. She had him back asleep in fifteen minutes and returned to the front to find Jack peering into a snow flurry.

"Do we need to pull over?" she asked, worried.

"Oh, no. This is nothing." He threw her an impudent grin. "I grew up in the mountains. I could drive in this stuff blindfolded."

"Let's not and say we did," she suggested nervously. To her, snow was something mysterious and possibly evil, despite all its beauty.

They were out of the storm and back in the clear in another few minutes, and she was able to relax. She watched Jack's hands on the wheel, large and strong and confident. Those hands had gently fathered four children and just as gently had made her feel like she'd never felt before. She had a soft spot for those hands. In fact, she downright loved them.

But that was only logical, as she loved the man with all her heart. She was getting used to the idea. At first, it had scared her. But now she was getting comfortable with this being-in-love stuff. If only she had a better idea of where it all might lead.

"What about you, Jack?" she asked him. "Once we get to Denver, what are you going to do?"

He glanced toward where the sky was turning purple as the sun began to make its presence known. "I'll spend some time staying with my parents, raising babies. I'm not just dumping them, you know. I plan to stay. As long as I can, at any rate."

She nodded, sympathy rising as she thought of how it would be to move back with her mother. "What would drive you away?" she asked softly.

He hesitated, as though this were something he didn't want to discuss with others. But when his eyes met hers and he saw the compassion there, he lost his inhibitions. "There will be difficulties. Actually, I hate doing this. It's like...like I'm using them."

"Your parents?"

He nodded.

"I'm sure they don't feel used."

He sighed, knowing that, too. "No, they've been urging me to do this all along. But they aren't young. Having four kids descend on them is going to change their quiet life into something resembling a carnival on speed. I hate to do it to them."

She nodded, liking his sensitivity to their feelings. "You feel guilty."

"You guessed it."

She turned and looked at him, loving his profile. "That's what parents are for, guilt trips," she told him lightly. "How else would we learn how to behave ourselves?"

He chuckled. "That's nice in theory, but hard to live with. Much as I love my parents, living with them is..."

"Difficult."

He nodded. "It was damn near impossible when I was younger. We'll see how it works out." He stretched his tired body in the comfortable seat. "Eventually, though, I'm going to go ahead with my plans of finding a little station in some Podunk town and taking control of my own little world."

"Running your own television station." She remembered he'd spoken of this before. "It sounds like a huge undertaking."

"Challenging, but not so huge. I've been thinking about it for a long time. Once I find the right place, I'll be ready."

She didn't talk again for a long time. Two pictures kept swimming through her mind, the first of Jack handling a shabby little station somewhere on his own, one baby on his knee while he spoke to the camera, two more playing at his feet, getting in the way of the cameraman, and Annie, sticking tapes into the monitor on cue from her father. The second picture was of a modern, efficient studio, superbly decorated, with the latest equipment on call and the most beautifully groomed and adept anchors doing their anchoring chores.

Which place would you rather be? a voice kept whispering in her ear. *Where do you think you would be happiest? Where would you make the most difference, be the most needed?*

The funny thing was that the people she imagined at the shabby little station all had smiles and the people she conjured up for her big-city edition were tense and smiled only when the red light was on in the camera.

Which place would you rather be?

They stopped to have breakfast at a fast-food outlet and the kids were thrilled with the unfamiliar fare. Baby Mack thought hash browns were the greatest and Kristi loved the pancakes. So did Annie.

"No little blue balls," she said, exalting as she popped a syrup-dripping bite into her mouth.

A woman at the next table laughed at some of the triplets' antics and said as she rose to leave, "You've really got a busload of babies there. You're a lucky couple. What a beautiful set of children."

Jack met J.J.'s gaze quickly, wondering how she would react to being considered the mother of this gang of four.

She smiled at him, beaming. *Hey,* her eyes told him. *It feels great.*

Before they left, J.J. called Sara to warn her that she and a "busload of babies" would be arriving shortly. Then they piled their babies back into the bus and off they went, heading for Denver.

"We're almost there," J.J. said softly.

"I know," Jack answered.

And that was all either of them said until they reached the top of the grade and the city was before them, glistening with a new coat of snow.

"Your friend's place is on this side of town," he told her. "My parents are on the other side. I guess we might as well drop you first."

"Okay," she said in a small voice. It sounded so final. And it was.

They both stared straight ahead, not saying anything for another mile or two. "Tell me about your friend Sara," Jack said at last. "What's she like?"

"Sara?" J.J. turned to him with relief. It was better to talk than to think right now. "Sara is tall and blond and beautiful and elegant. She's the sort of person you can imagine in charge of large things. She's just so cool and calm and...well, perfect. Everything she does is perfect. She even married the perfect man. And now, she's probably going to have the perfect baby."

"Doesn't all that perfection get a little annoying?" he asked dryly.

She turned to him and laughed. "You'd better be nice when I introduce you," she warned him.

"I'm going to get to meet this paragon of virtue, am I?"

"I never said she was all that virtuous," J.J. retorted. "The facade is the perfect part. As for the rest..." She shrugged her shoulders. "And, yes, you'll have to come in and meet her when we get there. After all, Annie needs a bathroom break and the babies could use a little exercise and maybe a cleanup before arriving on your parents' doorstep."

It was only moments later that they parked the van in front of Sara's house and began to unload the children. The babies crowed over the snow and Annie was enchanted by the house. Little by little, Jack and J.J. herded them toward the entrance, and suddenly the door flew open and Sara burst out, tall and blond and elegant as ever.

"J.J.! You made it!"

They embraced and laughed and Sara looked over her shoulder at the others. "My goodness, what a brood. Get those babies in from the cold."

The triplets would have been just as happy to stay outside and test their footing on the snow, but they were hustled inside the house and quickly found other things to capture their short attention spans. The room was filled with women, lots of nicely dressed ladies, milling and chatting and sipping punch. But all the triplets saw were legs, and occasionally a face peering down to mouth words like "How darling!" and "Oh, you precious thing."

They looked up the way country folk gaped at the tall buildings in the city, happy for the attention and just a little in awe. Annie was there with them at first, but then she was whisked away by someone who wanted to show her a stuffed pink flamingo. Jack and J.J. were busy talking to women who bounced and shrieked a lot. No one was paying much attention to the babies.

The triplets looked at one another. They were on their own. Very quietly, the babies left the room.

Meanwhile, J.J. was looking at her old friend and saying, "But, Sara, you're not pregnant. I thought—"

"Hush, I'll explain everything in due course. Right now I want you to see who else has already arrived."

"Cami! Hailey!" The four women cried out greetings as they rushed toward each other and joined in a group hug. Tears came to several eyes. It had been so many years.

"We were girls then," Sara said, looking from one to the other of her old roommates. "And now we're women."

"And Jack," said J.J., turning to bring him into the circle. "Meet Jack, everybody. He drove me here from Utah."

The three of them gazed at Jack appreciatively, and he returned the compliment with a rakish smile.

"I can hardly believe four such charming women could have been found at one college, let alone in one dorm suite," he said smoothly.

"Why, Juniper Joy, where did you find this wonderful man?" Hailey asked, laughing.

"Juniper Joy?" Jack's head whipped around and he looked at her hopefully. "Is that it?"

J.J. reddened. "Thanks a lot, Hailey," she said coolly. "He didn't know."

"Oops," said Hailey, chagrined. "It's so cute, J.J. I didn't realize you were keeping it a secret. I'm sorry."

"Juniper Joy." Jack grinned, visions of the teasing ahead filling his eyes with a sparkle. "I love it."

J.J. was about to make a smart remark back, but her attention was diverted by Annie, who was pulling on her shirttail. "J.J., come quick," she said, her little voice urgent. "The babies—"

J.J. gasped. "The babies!" she cried, looking about frantically. "They're gone."

Jack whirled, all humor erased from his face. "The babies," he muttered. "Where the hell are they?"

It seemed like only seconds since they'd had all three of them in hand, but now they were nowhere to be seen. Logic told him they couldn't have gone far, but cold panic roused itself in his chest anyway, especially since so many people jammed most of the rooms. There was no fear like the fear of losing a child.

"I'll check the stairs," J.J. said, turning toward the other side of the house.

"Okay," Jack said brusquely. "I'll take this direction."

He had no idea where he was going but then, neither did the babies, so he followed his instincts, striding quickly into the kitchen. The little knot of women chatting there turned and looked at him curiously.

"Have you seen three toddlers come through this way?" he asked hurriedly.

They shook their heads and looked at one another in question, then all started to talk at once, but he hurried on without answering. The next room was a den and it was empty.

"Damn it," he muttered, beginning to worry for real. "How far could they go?"

He turned a corner into the hallway, then on into the parlor, and his heart lurched. There was little blond Kristi sitting in the middle of a pile of presents that had been brought for Sara and her new baby. Kristi was too young to know these weren't for her. She liked the baby rattles and little toys attached to the ribbons. When she heard her father, she looked up and cooed happily and continued yanking off bows and peeling away wrapping paper in strips, her face wreathed in smiles of pure joy.

"No, Kristi, no!" he cried, looking down at the mess in dismay. There were scraps of paper and ribbon everywhere. He snatched her up out of the pile, ignoring her immediate change from cooing to whimpering. "Those aren't your presents and you're not allowed to do that."

Tucking her under one arm, he moved on into the family room, and there he found Kathy. She had climbed up onto a chair and was leaning over a large aquarium, reaching her tiny fist into the water, trying to catch a brightly colored fish that just flashed out of her grasp. Living aquarium seaweed clung to her hair like green strands, giving mute evidence to how her fishing expedition was going so far. Water dripped from her nose. She looked up and laughed with delight, a tiny river princess.

"Kathy!" He groaned, then grabbed her and curled her into his free arm and she shrieked, reaching back toward the fish who gaped at her as she left them.

"In here, Jack," J.J. was calling, and he followed her voice into the dining room. By now his anxiety had cooled, and he expected to find his little boy immersed in something just as he'd found the girls.

And he was right. He turned the corner into the room, and there was Baby Mack. He'd climbed up onto a chair at the table and was busy making mud pies out of the once-lovely white-and-yellow cake Sara had waiting for dessert time. Icing filled one ear and cake crumbs were smashed between his fingers. His mouth was a little red opening in a wall of yellow frosting. White icing laced his lashes.

Unfortunately, the room was ringed with spectators by now. Some were laughing, but most of the women looked aghast.

"Sara, I'm so sorry," J.J. was saying, trying to push cake back into a semblance of a rectangle with limited success. She looked up at Jack, her eyes anguished. "He can't have been in here longer than thirty seconds. How could he do so much damage?"

"It's no problem, J.J.," Sara said, although it was evident from the look on her face that it was a problem, indeed. After all, what she had on her hands now was hardly perfection.

J.J. snatched Baby Mack up by the waist as he squealed to get back to his delicious play dough.

"Which way to the bathroom?" she asked, sick at heart for the damage these children were inflicting on Sara's party. "Come on, Jack. Let's clean these babies up."

Annie came, too. They all headed for the bathroom, feeling like a family of outlaws. Once inside, J.J. turned on the faucet and took a washcloth and quickly began to clean the babies up. Jack joined her and they worked frantically for a few minutes, as though they could wash away what the babies had done.

Then for some reason their movements slowed, and finally they both looked up and met each other's gaze. They both looked like refugees from a range war. J.J.'s hair was straggling over her face. Jack's shirt was open and one shirttail was hanging out. They'd both ended up with frosting everywhere.

Their eyes met and they stared at each other, and suddenly they both burst out laughing. The laughter grew, and the babies joined in. Annie jumped up and down, giggling with delight. J.J. and Jack fell into an embrace that seemed to include everyone in the bathroom, and still they laughed.

"Did you see the look on Baby Mack's face when I pulled him away from that cake?" J.J. asked, gasping for breath.

"And you should have seen Kathy with the seaweed in her hair," Jack chimed in. "And Kristi. Wait until your friend Sara sees her artfully arranged stack of presents."

Annie chose that moment to say, "Look at what I have." She shoved it up at them. "I have a pink f'mingo. They said I could keep it."

J.J. laughed and hugged the little girl. "You're so good, Annie," she told her. "I don't know what we'd do without you to keep us on an even keel."

But by now, Baby Mack had caught sight of the stuffed pink bird, and he reached out his little arms, calling for it. Kristi and Kathy got a sudden yen for flamingos, as well, and in seconds, the three of them were demanding playtime in harmony.

Jack shook his head. He knew there was no hope for peace and quiet with this crew. He could only pray that he would survive the next few years—and then start practicing up for the teenage stage. But he would make it. It was a part of life, and he would love every minute of it. Especially if...

"J. J. Jensen," Jack said, grabbing her again and kissing a dab of frosting from her cheek, "Promise me one thing." He looked down at her, his eyes full of his feelings. "If things don't work out in New York, will you come back to us?"

"Jack Remington," she said, throwing back her head and staring straight up into his eyes, "You won't have to wait that long. I'm not going to New York."

His face changed. "What are you talking about?"

She smiled at him sweetly, all her love in her eyes. "I think I'm about to get a better offer," she said softly.

He frowned, not sure he got it yet. "Are you serious? Where?"

"Oh, I don't know." She laughed and reached up to clean a patch of icing from his nose. "Some small town in the Heartland, probably."

He still didn't dare take her words for what he thought she might mean.

"Are you saying ...?"

"Oh, Jack, will you get with it? I'm asking you to let me be a part of your dream. I want to help you with that TV station in the boondocks. I want to watch the triplets grow up and be there to make sure Annie gets a childhood." She put the flat of her hand against his cheek and shook her head, emotion filling her voice. "But most of all, I want you."

He stared at her, stunned, and then dropped a hard kiss onto her mouth. "J.J., you've got me," he said, his voice husky. "You've had me since the day I found you soaking in your hot tub."

She laughed, luxuriating in his embrace. "I wish you'd let me know."

"How could I when I wasn't even sure myself?"

She searched his blue gaze. "But you know now?"

"Oh, yes." His natural confidence was back, taking over. He knew it like he knew his own name. "I love you, J. J. Jensen. And I'd like to—"

"Don't say hire me to become a housekeeper," she warned.

He laughed, his eyes warm. "No. I want more from you than that, and you know it."

"Hush," she whispered. "The children are listening."

"The children?" He looked down. Only Baby Mack remained, and he was busy flushing something down the toilet. "Oh, my God," Jack cried. "Can you get him? But the girls..." He started for the door. "Where did they go now?"

"Find them," she ordered, grabbing the little boy and prying open his fist to find out what he planned to flush away next. Someone's car keys fell out onto the floor. "Oh, Jack, hurry. Get them quick."

"I will." He looked back and grinned, hesitating at the doorway. "Are you sure you know what you're getting into?" he asked her.

She grinned back, dangling the car keys from her finger. "I'm sure. I've never been so sure of anything in my life."

"I love you," he told her, turning to go after his errant daughters.

"I love you, too," she cried as he dashed off, then she grabbed Baby Mack before he could dive on into the water before him. "Every single one of you."

She pulled the child close and hugged him, tears of joy in her eyes as she felt his little chubby body relax in her arms.

"Every single one of you," she repeated.

And she finally knew what it was to feel complete.

*   *   *   *   *

*If you liked BABIES BY THE BUSLOAD,
don't miss INSTANT DAD, the fourth book in
Raye Morgan's exciting series,*
THE BABY SHOWER.
Coming this November!

This October, be the first to read these wonderful
authors as they make their dazzling debuts!

Women to Watch

THE WEDDING KISS by Robin Wells
(Silhouette Romance #1185)
A reluctant bachelor rescues the woman he loves
from the man she's about to marry—and turns into
a willing groom himself!

THE SEX TEST by Patty Salier
(Silhouette Desire #1032)
A pretty professor learns there's more to making love
than meets the eye when she takes lessons from
a sexy stranger.

IN A FAMILY WAY by Julia Mozingo
(Special Edition #1062)
A woman without a past finds shelter in the arms of
a handsome rancher. Can she trust him to protect
her unborn child?

UNDER COVER OF THE NIGHT by Roberta Tobeck
(Intimate Moments #744)
A rugged government agent encounters the woman he has
always loved. But past secrets could threaten their future.

DATELESS IN DALLAS by Samantha Carter
(Yours Truly)
A hapless reporter investigates how to find the perfect
mate—and winds up falling for her handsome rival!

Don't miss the brightest stars of tomorrow!

Only from ♥ Silhouette®
™

As seen on TV!
Free Gift Offer

With a Free Gift proof-of-purchase from any Silhouette® book,
you can receive a beautiful cubic zirconia pendant.

This gorgeous marquise-shaped stone is a genuine cubic
zirconia—accented by an 18" gold tone necklace.

(Approximate retail value $19.95)

Send for yours today...
compliments of ▼ *Silhouette*®

To receive your free gift, a cubic zirconia pendant, send us one original proof-of-purchase, photocopies not accepted, from the back of any Silhouette Romance™, Silhouette Desire®, Silhouette Special Edition®, Silhouette Intimate Moments® or Silhouette Yours Truly™ title available in August, September or October at your favorite retail outlet, together with the Free Gift Certificate, plus a check or money order for $1.65 u.s./$2.15 can. (do not send cash) to cover postage and handling, payable to Silhouette Free Gift Offer. We will send you the specified gift. Allow 6 to 8 weeks for delivery. Offer good until October 31, 1996 or while quantities last. Offer valid in the U.S. and Canada only.

Free Gift Certificate

Name: _____

Address: _____

City: _____ State/Province: _____ Zip/Postal Code: _____

Mail this certificate, one proof-of-purchase and a check or money order for postage and handling to: SILHOUETTE FREE GIFT OFFER 1996. In the U.S.: 3010 Walden Avenue, P.O. Box 9077, Buffalo NY 14269-9077. In Canada: P.O. Box 613, Fort Erie, Ontario L2Z 5X3.

FREE GIFT OFFER
084-KMD
ONE PROOF-OF-PURCHASE

To collect your fabulous FREE GIFT, a cubic zirconia pendant, you must include this original proof-of-purchase for each gift with the properly completed Free Gift Certificate.

084-KMD

The exciting new cross-line continuity series about love, marriage—and Daddy's unexpected need for a baby carriage!

You loved

THE BABY NOTION by Dixie Browning (Desire #1011 7/96)
and
BABY IN A BASKET by Helen R. Myers
(Romance #1169 8/96)

Now the series continues with...

MARRIED...WITH TWINS! by Jennifer Mikels
(Special Edition #1054 9/96)

The soon-to-be separated Kincaids just found out they're about to be parents. Will their newfound family grant them a second chance at marriage?

Don't miss the next books in this wonderful series:

HOW TO HOOK A HUSBAND (AND A BABY)
by Carolyn Zane (Yours Truly #29 10/96)

DISCOVERED: DADDY
by Marilyn Pappano (Intimate Moments #746 11/96)

DADDY KNOWS LAST continues each month...
only from

Silhouette®
™

Look us up on-line at: http://www.romance.net

DKL-SE